The Alpha Plague 4

Michael Robertson

Website and Newsletter:
www.michaelrobertson.co.uk

Email: subscribers@michaelrobertson.co.uk

Edited by:
Aaron Sikes - www.ajsikes.com
Terri King - http://terri-king.wix.com/editing

Cover Design by Christian Bentulan

Formatting by Polgarus Studio

The Alpha Plague 4
Michael Robertson
© 2016 Michael Robertson

The Alpha Plague 4 is a work of fiction. The characters, incidents, situations, and all dialogue are entirely a product of the author's imagination, or are used fictitiously and are not in any way representative of real people, places or things.

Any resemblance to persons living or dead is entirely coincidental.

All rights reserved

No part of this publication may be reproduced, stored in a retrieval system or transmitted in any form or by any means electronic, mechanical, photocopying, recording or otherwise, without the prior written permission of the author except in the case of brief quotations embodied in critical articles and reviews.

Would you like to be informed about my future releases?
Join my mailing list at:-

www.michaelrobertson.co.uk

Chapter One

Exhaustion seemed to treble the weight of Vicky's body as she stood on top of the shipping container, swaying while she looked down on the mob below.

With every passing minute, the crowd doubled. Before long, they wouldn't be able to see anything *but* the horrible fuckers. In every direction, it'd be miles and miles of diseased humans. At that moment, the darkness of night hid the worst of it. A shudder snapped through Vicky; God knows what it would look like in the morning.

Rhys walked over to Vicky and stood next to her. He said nothing as he stared out across the heads of the diseased. The monsters groaned and moaned below them. Their stench hung in the air so thick, Vicky could taste it as a stale tang on the back of her tongue.

After a deep sigh, Rhys reached across and placed a hand on Vicky's back.

She tensed at his touch. A lot had changed since she'd seen him last, and any contact felt wrong.

"Thank you for bringing my boy back to me."

Vicky shrugged and continued to stare down as she chewed the inside of her cheek. Black eyes stared up at her. Jaws snapped. Blood dribbled off chins.

Rhys then nodded out at the gathering horde. "The bastards may not be able to climb, but how the fuck will we get out of this?"

After a deep inhale, where the reek of rotten death damn near choked her, Vicky shrugged and gave Rhys the only answer she had. "Fucked if I know."

***

"So what are we going to do?" Larissa asked, her voice shrill, her tight face focused on Rhys as if he could produce some magic answer. Vicky ground her jaw as she watched the woman. It must have been the fifteenth time she'd asked that question in the past few hours. Larissa had apparently spent too much of her life as a princess. She'd be a fucking liability in this new world if she didn't start coming up with answers rather than questions.

Rhys didn't reply to her.

In the several hours that had passed since they'd climbed onto the shipping container, Vicky had stood up and sat down at least a dozen times. Each time, the other three looked at her as if she would provide them with an answer. Each time, she ignored their hopeful stares.

Rather than inspiration driving her actions, she rode the fumes of boredom. The hard container ached to sit on for too long, and if she remained stationary for the entire time, she'd go out of her fucking mind. At her lowest points, the sounds of the diseased grew so loud they damn near deafened her. If she didn't stand up, she'd get dragged down with them.

The start of a new day stretched into the still dark sky, turning the blackness above them ever so slightly grey. Hopefully daylight would bring a solution to their predicament.

As she stood on the container, Vicky rocked from side to side to ease the ache in her hips and stared at the horizon. Thank God for the warmer evenings. A biting winter chill through the night on top of everything else would have encouraged Vicky to launch herself into the crowd below. Hell, she'd already considered it a few times that evening—either that or throw Larissa over.

A glance at the other three, and Vicky and Larissa locked stares with one another. Not quite hostile, but Larissa could fuck off for all Vicky cared. From the slight narrowing of her eyes when she looked at Vicky, it seemed that Larissa felt the same way. Vicky glared long enough for it to be awkward before she turned away from the woman to look out over the vast swathe of diseased below.

The day grew lighter with each passing minute. The gradual illumination flooded Vicky with dread as it showed the crowd to be larger than she could have imagined. They'd amassed a rockstar-level following.

After she scoffed and shook her head, she looked down at the others. "This must have been how U2 felt when they filled a stadium. Not that their fans wanted to eat them like ours do." Vicky played air guitar to the crowd and snorted an ironic laugh.

The others remained silent. They clearly didn't see the humour in it. Vicky sighed and listened to the sound of perpetual suffering that rolled through the early morning exactly like it had rolled through the night. Each time the volume spiked with a shout or scream, Vicky jumped. No matter how often she heard it, she'd never get used to the sound of the monsters. The call of hatred and hunger ran ice through Vicky's veins. The fuckers below wouldn't stop until they'd taken them down.

"So what are we going to do?" Larissa said again, directing the question at Rhys.

After a shrug of his shoulders, Rhys opened his mouth, but Vicky cut him short. Still on her feet, she clenched her fists as she loomed over the woman. "All you've done is ask Rhys what are we going to do. Instead of asking the same question like a broken record, why don't you take some responsibility for coming up with some fucking answers?"

Larissa clapped her hands to the side of Flynn's head to cover his ears. "There's a little boy here. Can you *please* keep your language down?"

"Are you fucking serious?" Vicky pointed out at the thousands of diseased below them. "He's seen people eaten alive in the past day, do you seriously think a swear word is going to damage him? Jesus, Larissa, get a fucking grip. Instead of bitching and moaning, come up with a suggestion. Try to help the group rather than hinder it. This ain't a free ride anymore, princess, you need to pull your fucking weight."

With narrowed eyes that sent crow's feet to her temples, Larissa screwed her mouth up. "When you say 'the group', you mean *my* family, right?"

Heat flushed Vicky's cheeks. She kept her fists clenched and shook as she looked at Larissa. A glance at Rhys and it seemed obvious that he wouldn't get involved. Despite several deep breaths, Vicky's fury wound tighter with every passing second, and she spoke through clenched teeth. "Your family, which *I've* saved on two occasions. I stopped Rhys getting bitten *and* I brought your son back to you. Now don't get me wrong, the last thing I want to do is spend time with you, but in case you haven't noticed, we have a stadium full of diseased that all want to get at us, and my main concern is dealing with that. Believe me, I'll be gone the second I can get out of here, but that ain't an option at the moment. So how about we start thinking of solutions to our problems, yeah?"

Although Larissa opened her mouth to respond, Vicky looked away from her. She pulled her hair into a ponytail, so tight it stung the back of her head. To look at the bitch for much longer would lead to violence, and Flynn didn't need to see Vicky kick his mum in the teeth.

Vicky looked around and, with the onset of the greying morning light, saw something on top of one of the other containers. Without a word, she lifted the aluminium extension ladders they'd dragged up with them the previous night. She laid them across the gap that separated them from the other container.

The ladders clanged as she adjusted them, and it agitated the diseased more than before. They surged forward and kicked up a smell of rot. The sound of rolling thunder called out as hundreds of fists beat against the container, and the vibrations shook through Vicky's feet.

The containers had been laid out haphazardly, which left gaps between each one. Maybe Vicky could jump across, but there seemed little point when they had the ladders.

Exhausted from the day's insanity, Vicky's arms shook as she thrust them out to the side to get some balance.

The diseased roared louder the second Vicky stepped onto the ladder.

Vicky looked over her shoulder to see three exhausted faces watching her.

A deep breath and she turned back toward the other container. Her legs trembled with her first step, and she shook her head as if to fight the urge to look down. Pretty fucking hard when you have a collection of infected fuckers all reaching up and screaming their rage at you. Dark and glistening eyes bled as they focused on her. Snapping jaws. Cuts and gashes on faces and limbs. So many open wounds and bleeding orifices it scrambled Vicky's brain.

With the smell of rot came the distinct copper taste of blood. Vicky spat, but it did little to remove the metallic funk that lay against her tongue.

The ladder bowed slightly with Vicky's next step, and her legs shook worse than before. Without the diseased, she would have run across it with no problem. But the pit below her shook her resolve and spread doubt through her mind like a toxic mist.

A deep breath and Vicky lifted her head. She may have been unable to block out the smell and the sound, but she didn't have to look at them as well.

The ladder creaked with another step forward. Shiny still, it looked in great condition. The ladder would hold—of course it fucking would.

Vicky pushed on and took the final three steps before she

jumped off the other side and landed on the top of the container with a hollow *thud*. When she looked back at the others, she half smiled. None of them returned her gesture.

After she'd walked to the middle of the container, she stared down at the rusty tools that lay there; a pickaxe and sledgehammer. Vicky scanned around them. How the hell did they get up there? Then she saw the dents in the top of the container next to the tools. It looked like someone had tried to bust into one of the containers at some point. They must have abandoned the job before they got anywhere with it. Vicky lifted tools and waved them at the three on the other side. None of them seemed to get it.

When Vicky crossed back over the gap between the two containers, she moved with more confidence than the first time. The ladders would hold. Her steps called down to the creatures below and stirred up their fury again. Not that it mattered; they'd have even more noise to agitate them soon.

Back on the other side, Vicky held the tools up.

"What are they doing up here?" Rhys asked.

As she looked at the rusty tools, Vicky shrugged. "It looked like someone had used them to try to break into the container over there."

Three pairs of vacant eyes stared at her, so Vicky said, "I don't know about you three, but I can't stay up here all fucking day."

Although Larissa winced at yet another swear word, she kept it to herself this time, so Vicky continued. "If we can bust through into one of these containers, at least we can hide away for a time." A stamp of her foot made a hollow *boom*. "Maybe the floor will be flat inside this thing. At least, if we can get a bit more comfort, maybe we can rest up better and come up with a plan."

"Hardly an answer though, is it?" Larissa said.

With her stare locked on the half-naked woman, Vicky drew a deep breath. When she exhaled, her cheeks puffed out. "And you have a better idea, do you?"

When Larissa opened her mouth to reply, Vicky dropped the pickaxe. The loud *bang* drowned out the woman's retort and stirred up the diseased below. When Larissa tried for a second time, Vicky yelled and drove the sledgehammer against the top of the container. After the first savage swing, she stared straight at Larissa. She suddenly looked less interested in an argument. Vicky then lifted the sledgehammer above her head again and brought it crashing down once more. The loud *boom* rang out like a gong in the still morning air.

***

Covered in sweat from her last assault on the container, Vicky took the sledgehammer from the panting Rhys, filled her tight lungs with the rotting stench that surrounded them, and hit the same spot they'd both attacked for what felt like the thousandth time. The loud gong sounded again and a violent vibration ran up the handle, stimulating the aches in her tired shoulders.

Despite how many times they'd hit the container, the diseased below screamed with the same enthusiasm they'd had the first time they struck it. Insatiable in their desire to get at them, the diseased called out with their hellish and tormented cries.

Another loud clang and the container bent a little more than before. Vicky handed the sledgehammer to Rhys and grabbed the pickaxe. Although lighter than the sledgehammer, the weight of the tool still pulled on Vicky's sore arms.

With one wide-arching swing, Vicky drove the head of the rusty tool into the top of the container. The sharp spike pierced the metal, so she wiggled the pickaxe to make the hole bigger. Only a small breakthrough, but a breakthrough nonetheless.

***

It took at least another forty-five minutes to beat a large enough hole, but with perseverance, they did it.

The rattle of metal against metal called out as Vicky dragged the ladder back from where she'd used it as a bridge, and slid it into the hole. Although dark, the container had sounded empty when they hit it, so it came as little surprise to Vicky when the ladder struck the bottom before anything else.

A look at Rhys, Larissa, and Flynn caused Vicky to laugh at their pale faces and wide eyes. "I'll go in first then, shall I?"

When no one replied, Vicky laughed again and shook her head before she stepped onto the ladder and descended into the hole. She'd expected to be the first one into the container, but it would have been nice if someone had politely offered to go instead of her. But to do that would have risked her taking them up on their suggestion. And she would have sent Larissa down there in a heartbeat. Whatever happened, the container couldn't be any worse than what had gathered outside of it.

As Vicky delved deeper into the darkness, she caught a whiff of diesel. With her nose screwed up against the almost plastic reek, she kept going. Maybe she'd find a vehicle in the darkness.

Halfway down the ladder, Vicky pulled her lighter from her pocket and sparked it. The tormentor in her mind anticipated a mob of diseased, but the container sat mostly empty. Despite the smell suggesting otherwise, the floor of the container had a layer of stained plywood across it and nothing else. What looked like oil spills had soaked into the porous flooring.

Once inside the container—the banging from the diseased outside amplified because of the confined space—Vicky stood on the flat ground and let her eyes adjust to the darkness. The hole in the top let in enough light for her to see by, but Vicky sparked her lighter again anyway. As she walked across the container to the doors, the sound of her footsteps echoed in the dark space.

Tentative at first, she reached out to the doors and pushed. They seemed to be locked. Another shove, harder this time, and the doors didn't budge. With one last try, Vicky shoulder barged the doors and the solid resistance of them ran a shock through her body. They weren't giving in anytime soon. "Thank fuck for that."

After a quick check of the container, Vicky found some old gym equipment in one corner. A thick rope, soft enough to be the kind used in tug o' war, free weights, an old running machine, an exercise bike … Whoever had bought this lot had clearly given up on it some time ago. Either that or they had failed aspirations of being a personal trainer. As Vicky stood in the dark, the memory of the boot camp crowd flooded her mind. Black and cerise lycra, perfectly done hair and makeup … what had happened to those women? Had their vigorous weekly sessions set them up to survive in this new world?

Vicky walked over to the exercise bike and pushed down on the pedal. The wheel had seized up.

Vicky returned to the bottom of the ladder and squinted against the burn in her eyes as she looked up through the hole into the daylight. Three expectant faces stared down at her.

"It's fine down here."

"The doors are locked?" Rhys asked.

"Yep."

"And there's nothing of use down there?" Larissa asked.

Vicky shook her head. "No, I've found a rubbish collection of old gym equipment, but not a lot else. There's space and shelter down here. And the floor's flat. It's much more comfortable than up there."

"Okay," Rhys said, "we're coming down."

They passed Flynn down first, and Vicky took the small boy. Despite all the shit she'd taken from his mother already, she appreciated the little kid's spirit. A fighter, he rolled with the punches and even managed a smile as he descended the ladder.

When she lifted him off at the bottom, Flynn wrapped his arms around her neck and squeezed. The little boy smelled of dirt, smoke, and the diseased, but Vicky squeezed back like she'd never let go of him.

When his mum and dad made it down to the container, Larissa reached out to Flynn, who still hugged Vicky. If anything, he squeezed tighter.

After Vicky had tapped the back of his head, she said, "Come on, mate, your mum needs a cuddle."

But the boy didn't move.

For a moment, Larissa stared at her son. Her eyes glistened and her bottom lip twitched. A deep breath and she rubbed her eyes before she reached out and held the top of Vicky's arm. "It's okay. It's nice that you can offer him comfort. That's what he needs."

Before Vicky could reply, Larissa added, "Thank you for keeping my boy alive. Sorry, I've been a bitch up until this point. That'll change, I promise."

Vicky didn't reply as she watched Larissa walk away from her. When she looked at Rhys, the man offered her a tight-lipped smile before he followed his ex-wife to a dark corner, where they both sat down.

All the while, the boom of hands beat against the outside of the shipping container; a constant reminder of the diseased's intent. Not that they could forget it.

With the small form of the fragile Flynn in her arms, Vicky rocked him back and forth until he fell limp with exhaustion. At some point, he'd have to grow up. That point would be a lot fucking sooner than their previous society would have expected from a child of his age. Poor kid.

Chapter Two

The hard floor had turned Vicky's backside numb, and her shoulder blades ached from where she leaned up against the cold, corrugated wall of the container. With Flynn asleep on her lap, she hadn't moved for fear of waking him. Although, if she didn't stand up again soon, she'd seize up like a rusty hinge.

Despite having sat there for an entire day, Vicky hadn't been able to sleep; not even now the darkness of night had settled in again. The only light came from the moon through the hole in the roof. It somehow made the groan of the diseased, and their beating against the side of the container, even worse.

As the thud of pounding fists echoed through the dark space, Vicky ground her jaw and knocked the back of her head against the wall behind her. Despite the sharp sting of the contact, she continued, each whack harder than the last. Surrounded by the reek of diesel and with her hips aching from how she sat, Vicky let out a groan of her own. A long and continuous tone, it jumped every time she cracked the back of her head.

Fire burned in Vicky's knees, so she shifted to get more comfortable. Flynn snorted as her movement roused him.

Although he hadn't woken fully, it gave Vicky the motivation she needed.

In one fluid movement, Vicky rolled forward and stood up. Once upright, she wobbled for a second. After she'd found her balance, she bobbed up and down a couple of times. It eased the ache in her kneecaps and gave her the confidence to walk across the container as she carried Flynn back to his mum.

Larissa repeatedly blinked as she looked up at Vicky. She then adjusted herself to take her sleeping boy. As she held him in close, she kissed the top of his head, and her lips lifted with a slight smile.

With sharp stabbing pains at the base of her back and up each side of her ribcage, Vicky couldn't sit down again. Instead, she remained on her feet and paced the length of the dark shipping container. Five metres in length at the most, she walked to one side, touched the wall and felt the vibration from the diseased's fists, turned around and walked back again.

With each length of the container, she wound tighter than before. The *boom, boom, boom,* of the diseased cut to her core and pulled her shoulders to her neck. This couldn't go on. No fucking way.

After she'd paced another length, Vicky stopped at the gym equipment. The rope looked both tough and thin enough for what she needed. Vicky threaded it through one of the medium-sized free weights and tied it off to create a pendulum.

When she'd finished, she looked over to see that both Rhys and Larissa were watching her. She shrugged and pointed at one of the walls. "I can't sit in here with that going on outside. I *have* to do something." Her voice echoed in the enclosed space.

Vicky didn't wait for a response. She couldn't be bothered to explain her plan, choosing instead to simply act on it. Although it creaked beneath her weight, she climbed the ladder. At the top, she poked her head out into the night. The air reeked of rot, and it forced her tongue against the roof of her mouth in a dry heave.

Once she got out on the container, Vicky walked on tiptoes to the edge and peered over. Although she only had the moonlight, it showed her enough. The horde hadn't gathered around the container like they had when she'd seen them last. Hundreds of them still wandered in the airfield, but many had lost the target of their rage. Even those that still banged against the container seemed to do it by accident rather than design.

When Vicky, Rhys, Larissa, and Flynn had disappeared from their view that morning, the diseased must have eventually forgotten about them. Like small children, they seemed to have little understanding of where an object had gone if they couldn't see it anymore. Not that Vicky could do anything useful with that. Regardless of where they had their attention, they still surrounded her and would rip her limb from limb if she tried to get down.

As Vicky stood on the edge of the container, Rhys walked up behind her. "What are you doing?"

"You need to stand back," Vicky said as she let the weighted end of the rope hang down by about a foot. She then swung it around in a small circle, slowly at first, but picking up speed with each rotation.

After he'd shuffled forward again, Rhys repeated himself. "What are you doing?"

Vicky let more rope slide out so she could swing the weight in a wider circle. To maintain her balance, she had to bend her knees with each rotation. "We have to do something about these fuckers. I can't sit in that container and listen to them beat the shit out of it for days. We need to try to kill them."

As she let the rope out even farther, the circle now larger than her as she hung it off the edge of the container, Rhys backed away.

After she'd let out a little more length, Vicky dipped her knees to drop the weight low enough to catch the head of one of the diseased still close to the container. The heavy weight connected with its skull with a wet *pop*, which dropped it instantly. It upset the perfect circles she spun with the rope, however, and although she tried to control it, Vicky couldn't stop the weight from crashing with the shipping container. It killed the weight's momentum, unsettled her balance, and called out over the packed airfield like a gong.

As one, every diseased within sight turned to face Vicky. With her weighted rope limp, she froze. The low murmur of discontent sparked into a shrill cry of blood lust, and the pack rushed forward as one. Any space that had opened up between the diseased and the container closed instantly as they all pushed against one another to get near. With their rush forward the diseased brought a rich stench of rot and excrement with them. Vicky wrinkled her nose at the smell.

With Rhys still by her side, Vicky looked across at him to see him shrug. "It doesn't look like your plan worked, Vick."

"No shit." But it didn't stop her pulling the rope in and spinning a small circle with it again. After a few rotations, she let more of the rope out until it swooped down far enough for her to crack another diseased in the head.

Another loud cracking pop and the thing buckled beneath the blow. Within seconds, it had disappeared from view as the mob filled the space it left and trampled it beneath their feet. Clearly agitated by their fallen brethren, they screamed louder than before; a dreaded warning to Vicky that they'd get her.

After she'd dropped the third diseased, and it too vanished beneath the rush of its comrades, Vicky dropped the weighted rope down on top of the container and turned to Rhys. "Happy now?"

"Why would I be happy?"

"Because it hasn't fucking worked. Because it was a stupid idea to think I could kill the diseased from here with a rope and a weight." As she looked out over the crowd, she sighed. "We'd need a fucking nuclear bomb to remove this lot."

When Rhys didn't reply, Vicky slowly spun three hundred and sixty degrees to take in the airfield. Thick with diseased, the noise had called out to all of them.

Rhys looked as horrified as Vicky felt. He nodded toward the hole they'd made and said, "Come on, we need to get back inside the container and think of a better plan."

Vicky laughed. "There is no *better* plan, Rhys. We're fucked!"

***

Once back inside the container, Vicky stamped on the floor, sending an echo through the small space. "Fuck it!"

Instead of judgement, Larissa looked at her with concern

creasing her brow as Flynn stirred on her lap. "What's up?"

A shake of her head and Vicky paced the container again. "I thought I could kill some of the diseased, and it would give us a chance to escape from here."

"You *can't* kill them?" Larissa asked.

"I can kill them, but when I kill one, three more take its place. The commotion of killing one attracts others. I should have left it. When I went out there, they'd started to lose interest in the container. When they can't see us, they seem to forget about us. They …" Vicky clicked her fingers, and the sharp sound snapped through the small space. "That's it!"

This time, Rhys spoke up. "Huh?"

"I think I know how we can get away from here. Maybe not all of us, but I think a couple of us will be able to sneak out and get some supplies at least."

Chapter Three

With both Larissa and Rhys behind her, Vicky sat down on top of the container with Flynn and lifted the weight attached to the end of the rope. Despite having survived an entire day and night against the fuckers, Flynn still stared out at the horde of diseased with his jaw loose and his eyes wide.

"You don't need to worry about them, honey," Vicky said as she too looked out. The early morning sun stung her tired eyes from not having slept for the past few days. "They can't get you up here. They can't climb, and we're too high up for them to reach." Not that she could say with any certainty that they couldn't climb; only that she'd not seen any of them climb *yet*. A chill ran through her. Climbing diseased didn't bear thinking about.

When Flynn didn't reply, Vicky put a hand on his shoulder. "Do you hear me?"

After several blinks, the boy nodded and turned to look at her. Pale from what Vicky assumed to be a mixture of exhaustion, hunger, and fear, he still didn't speak.

"Okay," Vicky said as she held the weight with both hands,

"I need you to do this." She released her grip and let gravity do the work. A loud *boom* sounded out as the weight hit the container. More of the diseased looked up at them.

Flynn visibly shook as he stared out at the mob again.

With a hand on his shoulder, Vicky squeezed as she whispered, "Trust me, you don't need to fear them; not while you're up here."

For a second time, she lifted the weight and dropped it again. The noise stirred up the diseased, who grew louder as if agitated by the sound.

"I need you to have a go," Vicky said as she handed the weight to Flynn.

The boy nodded again but still didn't speak. He dropped the weight against the steel container and another loud *boom* called out.

As she watched Flynn lift the weight back up and hold it in mid-air, Vicky nodded. "Go on, give it another try."

Flynn dropped it again.

Without any encouragement, he did it again.

And again.

Vicky patted the slim boy's back. "Attaboy. Just keep that up. You'll get all of the diseased to come over to this side, and it'll give us a chance to get away. Remember, they can't hurt you up here, okay?"

After Flynn nodded, Vicky leaned forward and kissed the top of his head. The boy smelled of dirt, and his hair had turned greasy. When she looked back at his parents, she suddenly realised where she was. "Um … sorry."

Before Rhys could speak, Larissa shrugged. "What for?"

"For kissing him. It felt natural, but he's not my boy."

"You care about him. That's nothing to be sorry for."

Vicky dipped a slight nod at Larissa and got to her feet.

As Flynn beat a steady *boom*, Vicky lifted the ladder from out of the shipping container. Like she'd done to get the tools, she stretched it across the gap between the container they currently stood on and the closest one to them. At no more than two metres, the gap already seemed less imposing than it had the first time. The others' pale faces and tight expressions suggested they didn't feel the same.

"I don't think I can do it," Larissa said as she peered over the edge and shook her head.

With a hand on her back, Rhys leaned into his ex-wife. "You can. I know you can."

While the lovebirds worked it out, Vicky walked across the ladder with ease. Sure, Larissa's attitude had changed toward her, but that didn't stop her feeling like a spare part in this little family she'd found herself with.

Although Rhys moved with less confidence, his arms thrust out to the side and his attention on the diseased below, he followed Vicky over.

It looked like Larissa wouldn't come as she looked from Vicky and Rhys to Flynn, and back to Vicky and Rhys. "I don't want to leave him there by himself."

Rhys drew a breath to call across at her, and Vicky whacked him on the arm. With her finger pressed to her lips, she glowered at the man. She then pointed at Flynn and spoke in a whisper. "He's making the noise remember, not us."

Although she didn't call back, Vicky beckoned for Larissa to join them. With her hands pressed together as if in prayer, she spoke so only Rhys could hear her. "Please, come across. Flynn will be fine."

Several deep breaths later and a couple of false starts, and Larissa finally stepped onto the first rung of the ladder. A violent shake had a hold of her as she took each step at a time, but she did it nonetheless.

Once she'd made it to the other side, Vicky gave her shoulder a gentle squeeze and smiled at her.

Larissa looked back across at Flynn. "Are you sure this is the right thing to do? What if something happens to him?"

"He's safe there. Trust me. Besides, you're not leaving these containers. He'll only be metres away from you at the most."

When Rhys came over, the three of them huddled so tightly together Vicky could smell the stale sweat on the pair. She spoke in a low voice. "We need to get to the farthest container if we're to stand a chance. The good thing is, most of them have been placed close enough together for us to be able to jump across rather than use the ladder."

When Larissa's eyes widened, Vicky offered her a gentle smile. "You can still use the ladder if you like."

Larissa relaxed slightly.

***

In time, Larissa and Rhys moved across the containers with more confidence. So what if it had taken them at least five minutes on the first go.

Vicky glanced over at the small boy on the farthest container; his little back curved as he leaned over and used both hands to lift the weight and drop it down again. The monotonous *boom* tormented the diseased below, who twisted and writhed, their frustration clear to see.

When Vicky peered over the edge of the last shipping container, she saw a large chain-link fence pressed up against the back of it. She smiled. "This might just work, you know."

The back row of containers ran flush with the airport's perimeter fence. Free of diseased because they'd all been attracted to the noise, the fuckers wouldn't make it around that side even if they'd wanted to. There was no way through the fence. The field behind the airport would fill up at some point, but for now, it seemed clear.

When Vicky saw Flynn look over toward her, she gave him a thumbs up. The boy smiled and continued with his steady beat. The approval seemed to give him the will to continue.

As Vicky slid the ladder down into the field behind the airport, she spoke to Larissa. "You need to keep an eye out for us, okay?" From the containers, she could see the local town, and she pointed at it. "We're only a few hundred metres away from that built up area. There must be a shop or something there. We'll get in and get out quickly, so be ready for our return so you can lower the ladder again, all right?"

"But what about Flynn?"

"Go closer to him, sure," Vicky said, "but don't go right over because we need you to be able to get to us quickly when we return. Flynn knows he's safe there. I know he's only little, but the boy needs to grow up fast if he's to survive."

Larissa frowned at Vicky and her back stiffened. Telling another woman how to manage her son crossed a line, but they didn't have time for niceties. Flynn would be fine, and Larissa wouldn't need to be any farther away from him than where she currently stood.

When Larissa looked over at the boy, her shoulders slumped and she nodded. "Okay."

After the ladder had hit the soft ground of the field behind the airport, Vicky took one final deep breath and turned to Rhys. "You ready for this?"

Pale-faced, Rhys gulped. "As ready as I'll ever be."

And with that, Vicky climbed down the ladder into the field. The wind ran across the open space and crashed into her as she looked out over it. It seemed free of the diseased …

For now.

Chapter Four

By the time they'd walked about fifty metres into the field, the dew had soaked through Vicky's trainers, and her feet squelched as she walked. Exposed in the open space, she moved as quietly as she could, gripped her telescopic baton so tight her knuckles hurt, and listened to the sounds of the diseased just metres away.

A thick tree line separated Vicky and Rhys from the vast horde of diseased that were all being drawn to Flynn's beat against the container. The stench of decay and human shit thickened the air to the point where Vicky felt like she could taste it. Despite the urge to spit, she resisted. She didn't need to make any extra noise, and with a heave locked and loaded as it pushed up against her throat, any stimulation in that area of her body and she'd vomit for sure. If hawking up a bit of phlegm didn't attract the diseased ….

The town that they'd seen from on top of the containers didn't look far away. A five-minute walk maybe. Although, with a horde as large as the one in the airport, five minutes away felt like the other side of the planet. With her pulse on overdrive, Vicky scanned the ground she trod. One snapped twig, a sneeze, hell, even a startled animal could alert the masses.

Although they hadn't previously agreed on it, the pair resorted to silent communication. When Rhys looked over at her again, Vicky pointed at her eyes and then pointed to the tree line. They needed to keep an eye out. If just one of the diseased saw them, their plan would have to change in an instant. Not that she needed to tell Rhys that; judging by his wide eyes and twitchy head movements, he seemed more than aware of the fact.

Every roar and scream spiked Vicky's pulse even though none of the sounds had been directed at them—so far.

The *boom* of Flynn's weight against the top of the shipping container rang out with such a steady beat, Vicky marched in time with it. One, two, three, *boom*. One, two, three, *boom*. It felt like a death march.

As Vicky scanned the hedge line, she saw a part where the trees thinned a little. The farther they got from the containers, the less diseased there were, but she could still see plenty of the fuckers milling about on the other side. Without a word, she grabbed a handful of Rhys's shirt sleeve and dragged him closer to the tree line.

When he resisted, Vicky leaned close to him. "The trees are thinning out. We need to get past the gap without being seen."

"And getting closer to them will achieve that?"

"The trees will hide us. The closer we are to them, the shorter distance we have to be exposed for. If we stay out in the field, they'll be able to see us for much longer when we cross the gap."

Although he came with her when she tugged on his sleeve again, Rhys looked far from convinced as the pair of them moved close to the tree line.

The smell when they'd walked in the field had nothing on the stench that rose as they got closer to the mob. The heave Vicky already had in her throat, forced her tongue against the roof of her mouth, and she coughed slightly to clear it. It had little impact.

The scrape of feet and moans of agitation stirred on the other side of the hedge. The sound of Flynn's repetitive beat clearly riled them, even from this distance.

When they got to within about a metre of the tree line, Vicky led the way along it until they came to the gap. She turned to Rhys. "We have to dart across this space *together*. We'll be visible for the shortest time that way. What do you think?"

"I think there has to be another way."

After she'd looked out across the huge open field, Vicky turned back to Rhys and threw her hands up in a shrug. "Well, what is it then?"

With his mouth hanging open slightly, Rhys looked across the field too. Once he'd turned back to Vicky, he said, "We'll do it on the count of three, yeah?"

Vicky nodded.

"One," Rhys said.

"Two."

Just as he finished the second count, Vicky saw it, and she also saw that Rhys hadn't.

"Three."

As he darted out across the gap, Vicky hooked her arm around his neck, dragged him back, and pulled him to the ground with her. Although he squirmed, he thankfully knew not to shout. A second later he fell limp when at least fifteen of the fuckers sprinted past the gap in the hedge, less than a metre away from where they would have been.

Once they'd passed, Vicky let go of him and stood up again.

When Rhys got to his feet, he nodded at her. "Thank you. I didn't see them at all."

"I know. Let me count it down, yeah?"

Rhys flushed red, but his ego didn't matter one jot at that point. He could lick his wounds when they returned to the containers with food and drink.

Vicky counted down in her head instead of out loud and reached back to grab Rhys. All the while she watched the gap in the trees. *Three, two, one.* A tug on Rhys's sleeve and the pair of them sprinted across the small space, almost silent save for the rustling grass at their feet.

***

With their walk tightened by a path that led from the field, the pair continued in the direction of the town. Penned in by a vast building on one side—which looked like a hanger for private jets—and the thick tree line of the airport on the other, Vicky sped up in the direction of what looked like a road at the end. Flynn's banging accompanied them as they walked down the narrow alleyway.

"Were it not for that noise," Vicky said in a whisper, "I don't think we would have made it across that gap."

After he'd looked back in the direction of the containers, Rhys turned back to Vicky and chewed on his bottom lip. "I'm not sure that's a good thing, though."

"You *wanted* us to be seen?"

"Of *course* not. I just don't like the idea of an entire fucking town of diseased staring up at my son."

He had a point, and Vicky nodded. "They can't get to him, though. And when we come back, we can hide out for a while in one of the containers. They'll all go away soon enough. They seem to lose interest pretty quickly."

The pair walked in silence for a few seconds before Rhys said, "Um …"

Vicky looked at him.

"That, um … that kiss."

"It's all right, Rhys. You—"

"No, I do need to talk about it."

Because she walked ahead of him, Vicky faced the direction they were travelling in and shook her head as he spoke.

"Well, things are different now than they were. With everything that's happened, I think I should try to stay single for Flynn's sake."

The words stung and it caught Vicky off guard. Why did she give a fuck about Rhys and his rejection? Maybe it was more down to what they'd been through than anything. "Look, Rhys, it was a kiss. Get over yourself, yeah? Fucking hell, mate, no need to go overboard." Heat flushed her cheeks, so she continued to stare straight ahead.

***

The end of the alley marked the end of the airport's boundaries. The space opened up onto a two-lane road with a petrol station no more than fifty metres away, and another field directly opposite them. A quick scan of the area and it seemed clear.

When Rhys stepped out next to her, Vicky nodded diagonally across the road at the petrol station. "I think we've found what we're looking for."

Although distant, the boom of Flynn's weight continued to call out. Too much longer and some of the diseased from the town may appear, so Vicky grabbed Rhys's sleeve again and led him across the road at a jog.

The hard concrete and the cover of the petrol station's roof amplified the pair's footsteps as they ran up to the glass front door. As she moved, Vicky raised her telescopic baton and kept her eyes peeled for signs of the diseased.

At the door to the petrol station, Vicky looked through the window. It had to be reinforced glass and would take more than one whack with the baton to get through it. They'd made it that far. If they got in and out, maybe the noise wouldn't matter. As Vicky stared into the shop, she rocked on the balls of her feet. Two nights without sleep and her body had turned to lead. Just before she attacked the glass with her first blow, Vicky pushed the door. It swung open. She laughed, and when she spoke, her words dragged from tiredness. "Of course the place would be open. Why would everywhere be abandoned and locked up? The disease hit at lunch time."

"Huh?" Rhys said. When he glanced up, his expression hung loose. He looked as tired as Vicky felt.

"Don't worry," Vicky said and stepped into the petrol station.

After Rhys had followed her in, Vicky closed the door and found a twist lock on the inside. A quick turn and the bolt made a *snap* as it slid into the frame.

Vicky's heart damn near exploded when she looked up to see a diseased sprint across the forecourt. It had come from nowhere. Vicky moved back several steps before it collided with the glass door with a loud *bang*!

The door held.

Out of breath from panic, Vicky watched the creature press its face to the glass and smear blood all over it as it bit and snapped its teeth at her. It hadn't just appeared … they'd both missed it. Why didn't they wait until they felt more rested to come out and get supplies?

When she turned to see Rhys had frozen as he stared at the creature, Vicky laughed and rubbed her sore eyes. "At least the door held."

Rhys nodded, his face slack and his vision glazed as he focused on the raging diseased just metres away.

"There must be a back exit," Vicky said. "Let's get a couple of bags of supplies, and then we'll find it."

***

A quick check behind the sales counter and Vicky found a stack of carrier bags. She double bagged two, gave one of them to Rhys, and kept one for herself. Within a few minutes, they'd filled their respective bags. They'd taken as many fresh items as they could. Best to use that food before it all went off.

With a tacky throat from all the running, Vicky sipped on a fresh water. The cool liquid quenched her thirst, although it couldn't dispel the exhausted fog in her mind. Despite her urge to swig the entire bottle, she dropped it back in her bag after just a couple of sips. A stomach full of water wouldn't help her run back to the airport one fucking bit.

Vicky nodded at the door in the wall behind the till. "You wanna check in there and see if there's a way out? It looks like it leads to a storeroom." She nodded at the front door with the diseased pressed up against it. "I'll keep this fucker entertained."

As seemed to happen with the diseased, once one picked up the scent of something, it didn't take long for their mates to join in. When Vicky caught movement on the other side of the road, she looked past the diseased directly in front of her to see a crowd of about ten of the horrible fuckers.

Each one ran with their clumsy gait as they crossed the forecourt and crashed against the door one after the other. Logic told Vicky the door would hold, but that didn't stop her flinching with every collision, her legs so weak she nearly fell to the ground a couple of times.

With the fuckers pressed up against the glass, wide bloody eyes and dark drooling mouths, Vicky glanced to see Rhys open the door to the storeroom. When one of the diseased also looked his way, Vicky punched her side of the glass so hard it stung her fist. The mob on the other side roared in response.

"I'm here, you dumb fucks!" Vicky banged her fist against the reinforced glass again. "Look at me, you stupid bastards."

Several more diseased ran into the forecourt and pushed the existing mob harder against the door. Despite the sounds of chaos and fury directed at her, Vicky had more of her attention on the door Rhys had disappeared through than the one in front of her. They hadn't checked in there before she sent him in. *They hadn't fucking checked!*

Vicky put her bag down, held her baton out in front of her and stepped toward the storeroom.

When Rhys poked his head out, she nearly swung for him, her heart in her mouth as she said, "*Fuck!* I thought you were one of them."

"Thanks!"

A shake of her head and Vicky nodded behind him. "How's it look in there? You find a way out?"

Rhys nodded. "Yep. There's a door that leads out the back of the place, and I couldn't see any diseased when I checked out there."

"Okay," Vicky said. "You go and open the back door, and I'll make sure this lot stay here. I'll be right out after you."

Rhys paused for a second as he looked at Vicky, but then turned around and headed back to the storeroom.

The moment he vanished from sight, Vicky hurried back over to the front door and shook it. She watched the frenzy spark outside as she picked up her carrier bag. Wide mouths issued sharp hisses. Bleeding eyes remained fixed on her and glistened; they were active, yet strangely detached in their dead glare. Several more diseased joined the pack, which totalled about twenty by now. One last bang on the door and Vicky flipped them the bird. "Fuck you, you fucking pieces of shit." She then made for the storeroom.

Although dark in the small room, Rhys had the back door open, allowing the space to be lit up enough for Vicky to move through the maze of shelves as she headed for the light. She knew Rhys and knew she *could* trust him, but if he felt anywhere near as tired as she did, *should* she trust him at that moment?

What if he'd made a mistake? What if he hadn't seen that one diseased that would end her?

When she stepped out the back of the petrol station, Vicky scanned around. It stood empty and the sounds of the diseased around the front of the building called out as they still clearly tried to get in through the front door.

***

The pair took the long way back through a field that ran parallel with the road to avoid Vicky's fan club in the petrol station's forecourt. Their bags rustled as they walked. When they came out on the road, Vicky scanned both ways before she led them across to the alleyway that ran alongside the airport.

Vicky watched Rhys climb over the stile ahead of her. Halfway over herself, and a tickle burned in her nose. With watering eyes, panic washed over her. Before she could control it, she sneezed so hard her entire body bucked, and the sound of it rang through the still air. The collection of diseased in the petrol station's forecourt turned to her as one. Ice ran through her veins, and she looked at Rhys. "Run. Run now!"

Chapter Five

Ten years later.

The *boom* of the weight against the shipping container provided some comfort for Vicky as she pushed on, her body tired from years of supply runs. With Rhys behind her, the pair sprinted up the alleyway toward the field at the back of the airport. Several diseased chased after them, their breaths heavy and their feet clumsy against the ground. Although their numbers had thinned, a considerable amount of the fuckers had learned how to hunt and survive. They ate berries and animals. Surprisingly composed when it came to hunting, they still lost their minds in the presence of humans. Consumed with a desire to get at Vicky and Rhys, they moved as fast now as they had ten years previously.

When she got close to the stile that led out into the field beside the airport, Vicky jumped up onto the step and hurdled the fence. She'd meant to knock the barrier down some time ago, but something more important always came up.

The amount of diseased may have dwindled over time, but a

large crowd of them still gathered at the airport on the other side the tree line. They smelled worse than ever. They may have learned how to hunt and survive, but none of the fuckers knew how to wipe their arse. Every single one of them stood covered in piss and shit.

Vicky estimated it to be May. The sun shone brightly in the sky, and with the winter behind them, they'd entered a time of growth. It had been a long few months, and Vicky now had to tie her trousers extra tight to prevent them from falling. But now the first signs of vegetables grew in their patch by the containers, and she could feel her strength returning.

Without breaking stride, Vicky gasped for breath as she looked over her shoulder at the diseased on their tail. A quick count and it looked like six, maybe seven of them. The fuckers ran as fast as ever. It seemed like Vicky and Rhys would lose their speed before the diseased did. The original plan of waiting for them to die out had failed. At some point, the tables would turn, and the diseased would have the edge.

Vicky looked at Rhys. Red-faced and with his mouth open wide, he gasped for breath and nodded at her. They'd done this a thousand times; they could do it again. It didn't matter that the diseased had gotten closer to them today than they had in a long time; they could do it.

With the swish of the long grass as it tugged on their feet, and the fury of the diseased both behind them and on the other side of the fence, Vicky clenched her jaw and pushed on.

A small rucksack on her back, it had gotten lighter every time they returned from a supply run. Back in the day, she'd be able to pack the thing to busting and would get bruises from running with it. The diseased may have been good at catching dogs, rabbits, squirrels … hell, they even knew what berries to eat, but the fuckers couldn't open a tin or a bottle, so the world still had something to offer. Sure, most of it had gone off, but it still tasted okay—well, some of it did at least. The water remained drinkable, and it rained enough for them to catch the extra they needed.

Dressed in no more than rags, the diseased continued on their tail. Most of them had their torsos exposed, and their trousers or skirts ripped off from mid-thigh down. Dried blood filled their eye sockets. The fuckers shouldn't be able to see, yet they picked up a scent and moved with utter confidence as they homed in on it.

Vicky's feet shifted and adjusted over the hard and uneven ground. Although she knew the run well, one slip and she'd be fucked.

As they rounded the bend toward the back of the containers, the *boom* sounded louder, and they saw Flynn. He stood at the top of the ladder. Tall for his age, and lean, he may not have left the containers in the past decade, but he'd worked out every day in anticipation of it. Boredom had set in quickly, so they set up the gym equipment in the container they'd found it in, which gave both him and Larissa somewhere to exercise; one of the many things they'd done to stave off the madness of cabin fever.

With a five-metre lead on Rhys and about a fifteen-metre lead on the diseased, Vicky pushed on. Without missing a beat, she jumped onto the ladder and climbed it like a monkey up a tree. She leapt past Flynn and landed flat against the container with a resounding slap.

As she got to her feet, she fought for breath and watched Rhys. The distance between him and the lead diseased had shrunk to no more than a metre or so. The rest of the pack still hung back far enough for him to get away. But if he stopped to fight the one at the front, he wouldn't make it.

Before Vicky could speak, Flynn lifted a rock from the top of the container. With the cry for him to stop caught in her throat, Vicky watched him launch it at his father and the lead diseased directly behind him. It connected with the diseased's head with a loud *crack* and knocked it to the ground.

A few seconds later, Rhys jumped onto the ladder and climbed it. When he got to the top, Vicky helped Flynn pull the ladder up after him just in time for the rest of the pack to reach out for it and miss. The shudder of seven bodies crashed into the container below, and the vibrations shook through Vicky's feet.

Rhys lay on his back with his mouth open wide and stared up at the sky. Sweat glistened on his red face, and his slim ribcage rose and fell with his heavy breaths.

Larissa's war drum continued, unrelenting in the background as a steady *boom, boom, boom.*

Chapter Six

As Vicky stood with her hands on her hips, she pulled deep breaths into her tight lungs and watched the diseased on the ground below. The one Flynn had hit with the rock lay sparked, and fresh blood ran down its twisted face from an angry gash across its forehead.

The sound of Rhys's heavy breaths joined the moans and groans of the diseased. Catching her breath, Vicky watched him lie on top of the container next to the ladder they'd pulled up after him.

When Rhys looked up at her, he drew another deep breath and slowly got to his feet. Still puffed out, he stood for a moment to compose himself before he put an arm around his son. "Well done, mate."

Flynn pulled his long and greasy hair away from his face and smiled at his dad.

Over the years, Vicky and Rhys had found extra ladders. Enough that they had one for every gap that needed one, and one leading down into each of the containers. Seventeen in total, each container had a hole in the top of it and had been converted into either a storage space, a place for communal use, a bathroom, or a bedroom.

At sixteen, Flynn still bunked in with his parents. Vicky had moved into her own container the second she could. After several years, she'd finally managed to get a decent night's sleep through the banging and groaning on the other side of the steel walls. Now she barely heard the horrible fuckers.

Vicky watched Larissa, who continued to bang the weight against the container. When Larissa finally looked up, Vicky waved for her to stop. Larissa placed the weight down and stood up. She pressed her hands into her kidneys and pushed her stomach forward as if to ease the aches from her body. As Vicky watched her, she felt her pain. The older she got, the longer her aches persisted. Most days she woke up tired and went to sleep exhausted.

With Flynn and Rhys following behind her, Vicky moved from one container to another as she headed for the one they used as a kitchen.

"Did you see that, Dad?"

"I did, mate, you scored a direct hit. I'd be dead were it not for you."

As she hopped across a small gap of no more than a metre wide, Vicky looked down at the snapping jaws of the diseased wedged into the tight space below. Rhys and Flynn followed after her, more focused on their conversation with one another than the mindless killing machines around them.

The sound of Flynn's footsteps then rushed up to Vicky until he fell into stride next to her. "Did you see that, Vicky? Did you see the shot?"

With her attention on the ladder that stretched across another, larger gap, Vicky walked across it and didn't respond.

After he'd followed her over, Flynn caught up with her again. "I said, did you see me?"

"I *heard* you."

When Flynn stopped dead, Vicky did too. A little abrasive at first, she softened her tone. "It was a good shot, but maybe a lucky one."

Rhys had caught up with them and looked at Vicky. "Why don't you give the kid a break, Vick? He did well."

Heat rushed to Vicky's cheeks as she pointed at Flynn. "Because he doesn't need a break. He needs to be *better*. The kid's nearly sixteen. He's nearly a man, and we're praising him for the occasional lucky shot. He's fitter than all of us and should be on supply runs with us. But instead, you're treating him like a baby by not putting any expectation on him to even try to get good enough to do a supply run."

Before Rhys could respond, Flynn stepped toward Vicky. "But that was for real then. I just saved Dad's life with that shot. I *am* good enough to come out with you guys, so let me come."

Although he looked at Vicky, Vicky said nothing. Instead, she turned to Rhys.

The warm glow of biased parental praise left Rhys's face. Suddenly he'd been called out on his son's abilities. He sighed and dropped his head. "You're not ready yet, mate."

"But, how will I get ready if you don't take me out with you, Dad?"

"He's right, you know," Vicky said. "Sooner or later, you're going to have to trust him enough to let him come. We're all getting older; we need to adapt to that, not stagnate."

Rhys opened his mouth to reply, but Vicky didn't give him a chance. Instead, she spun on her heel and walked toward the kitchen container. They'd run far for the bottled water and fresh vegetables Vicky had in her backpack. Time they fucking ate it rather than just stood around talking in circles.

Chapter Seven

"Don't suppose you've found any more paint?" Flynn said to Vicky as the four of them sat in the dining room container. Like all of the other containers, it had a hole in the roof to access it, and the inside had been painted. Vicky looked at the crude rendering of a city skyline with a sun behind it. Flynn had used a lot of bright colours in the dark space. Rhys found paint years back and brought it for Flynn. Since then, the boy had been obsessed. Before long, paint became a supply as important as food and water. Whenever Vicky questioned the extra weight on the supply runs, Rhys would tell her that it fed Flynn's soul; that his spirit needed as much, if not more, nourishment than his physical body.

The second Vicky finished her last mouthful of stewed potato and peas, she stood up and nodded at Larissa, Rhys, and Flynn. "Thanks for the meal, guys. I'm going to go back to my container."

Before Vicky could walk away, Flynn asked, "Why don't you hang out with us anymore?" His voice echoed in the enclosed space.

"What do you mean? I *do* hang out with you. What have we just done?"

"Yeah, but once you've eaten, you always go back to your container."

Of course she did. A smart kid, Vicky didn't need to lie to him about it. But maybe she didn't need to tell him the truth either. Not yet.

"I dunno," she said. "I get a lot more tired now than I used to. I need more rest." Not a lie, but in her mid-thirties, not the entire truth either. She had a lot of life left in her yet. She just needed to find a reason to live it.

So he didn't have any more of an opportunity to quiz her, Vicky turned her back on Flynn and climbed the ladder out of there. The slap of her steps against the aluminium rungs called out as the only sound.

When Vicky poked her head from the container, the smell of stew vanished and she entered a reek of decay and shit. As she stood up high, she looked down at the diseased. A dense crowd for sure, but not like back in the day. The first day they'd arrived, the horrible fuckers filled the entire airport. Only a small airport, Biggin Hill had been great during the Second World War, but not since then. Other than private jets and air shows, the place had been left as a memory of what it used to be. Like a working museum.

Despite its size though, it still took up enough space that when filled with diseased, it painted an intimidating picture. Once in the thousands, they numbered maybe two hundred now. All of them looked up at Vicky the second she appeared, and agitation ruffled through the crowd.

Vicky stood above the monsters for a moment longer and stared down at them. She then looked out over the small airport. The once smooth tarmac had broken up, and grass grew through the cracks. The place would be hard to drive a car across now, let alone land an aeroplane on.

The setting sun hit her face as the heat of a new season prickled against her skin. A deep inhale and Vicky caught the slightest whiff of something fresher than the shitty air.

As she made her way toward her container—the one as far away from the others as she could be—she felt for the wind-up radio in her pocket. Nobody knew she had it. A small thing, but because she'd shared everything for the past decade, she needed something of her own. She'd had it for months now. If she'd have given Flynn the true answer as to why she went back to her container early, she would have had to show him the radio.

***

After Vicky had descended into her container, she lay down on the pile of blankets she called a bed, and she pulled her boots off her feet. Sore from the day, she wriggled her toes to ease the beginnings of cramp. Vicky never let anyone in her container, and no one questioned it. Because they had to live on top of one another, they respected Vicky's need for space. Had they come here, they would have asked questions.

Vicky looked at the paint cans that she stacked in the corner years ago, and then at the plain walls. As the only container that hadn't been decorated, they would definitely ask questions. To paint the place would be to accept it as home. In all the years they'd been there, Vicky hadn't ever felt prepared to do that. A deep sigh and she pulled the small wind-up radio from her pocket.

Made from clear, green plastic, the device sat in the palm of her hand. About the size of a cigarette box, it had a small black handle on the back that Vicky wound, less cautious of the clicking noise than she had been in the past. At least if they heard it, it could encourage some more open discussion … even if they did see her undecorated container. Maybe they'd accept she needed to move on.

With the frequency on its usual setting, Vicky listened to the recorded message. It had changed today. It changed every few weeks.

"Home is a place where we're beginning to fight back. It's been over ten years since the outbreak, and the tactic of hiding isn't working. We need to build an army. We need to fight back against the diseased. We have plenty of people already. We have running water and warm showers. We have electricity and food to go around. All we ask is that you believe the same as us: that we need to fight back. Ablebodied or not, we will take you in, but you need to share our vision. Home is located just near Britnall. The diseased can't read, so we have signs to guide the way. Everyone is welcome. Please come and join us."

The message repeated itself and Vicky listened to it again before she turned the radio off and slipped it back into her pocket. The messages had been consistent with their proposed agenda for as long as she'd listened to them. Although the idea had been similar in each message, it had changed several times in the few months that Vicky had had the radio for. They must have people like Vicky all over, people who needed convincing that Home was the place to go. At least if the messages changed, it proved that an actual person would be waiting for them.

As she laid her head down, Vicky listened to the amplified beat of the diseased on the outside of her container. She could have picked a container in the middle of several others, but not only did she need her space, she needed to remember what they faced. Even when she slept, she needed the reminder of what would happen to her should she lower her guard.

With the roars and groans of the enemy outside, Vicky hugged the radio to her chest and listened.

Chapter Eight

As always, Vicky led the way out of the alley with her catapult pulled taut and held out in front of her. A crack shot, in a country where there were very few guns, she could give them the advantage, no matter how small.

A quick look up and down the road, and she saw a rabbit sitting on the petrol station's forecourt. Like with every other road and pavement, grass had pushed up through the hard crust as nature reclaimed the world for its own. The petrol pumps, useless years ago after all of the fuel had evaporated, had turned green from the moss and vines that climbed them. Despite the long grass, the rabbit—oblivious to Vicky's hungry eyes fixed on it—sat exposed in the forecourt. Even from the twenty or so metres away, Vicky could knock a stem of grass from its mouth if she chose to.

Vicky glanced at Rhys, who'd stopped behind her. With the catapult's elastic pulled taut, she drew deep breaths to still her pulse, closed one eye, and focused on her target.

When her heart rate settled, Vicky let go. The *twang* of the catapult sounded out, the stone scored a direct hit on the rabbit's skull, and the creature fell to the ground. When a quick check up and down the road for diseased showed her none, she jogged toward the small creature.

The catapult had often been enough to stun the creatures, but Vicky had had many small animals spring to life when she grabbed them. Before the rabbit could even think about it, she lifted its warm body and pulled its neck until it popped.

With the rabbit limp, she tied some string around its neck and fastened it to her belt.

Rhys caught up with her, looked down at the limp creature, and nodded at Vicky with a smile. "Good work."

Vicky nodded back while she looked at the petrol station. The windows had been smashed from a time when they'd thrown rocks through them to distract the diseased. The shelves had been picked clean of most things other than air fresheners and screen wash. "To think, this place was full of food ten years ago."

As Rhys exhaled, his cheeks puffed out. "I suppose we should celebrate the fact that we've survived for this long."

"Yeah, although, what I would give to have a shop full of chocolate again. I'd literally kill for a Snickers now." Just the mention of it made Vicky's mouth water. She swallowed, her throat dry from dehydration. She hadn't had a drink that morning, and the slight pinch of a headache squeezed her temples.

Before Rhys could respond, Vicky said, "When will you bring Flynn out?"

Instantly defensive, Rhys straightened his back and his voice rose in pitch. "He's a *boy*."

"A young man."

"*Sixteen*, Vicky! When did you have to take responsibility for yourself? I bet it was older than sixteen."

"Actually, it wasn't. I was on my own the second my old man died, but that's beside the point. In case you haven't noticed, we don't live in a world of shit television schedules and central heating anymore. Kids have to grow up quicker nowadays. That's just the way it is."

As he shook his head, Rhys chewed the inside of his mouth. A deep frown crushed his brow. "Not yet. Not now. The boy's too young."

"He's in better physical shape than we are. Not that you've let him off the containers, but I wouldn't mind betting he could outrun any of us. He'll never be ready for this world if you don't give him a chance. Heaven forbid, but we might not come back one day. And what then? Larissa is all he'll have left, and you won't have prepared him to survive. I would have started with him a couple of years back."

"Yeah, well you're not me, are you?" Rhys said.

"No." Vicky shook her head. "No, I'm not."

The silence hung between the pair for a moment. Although the sun shone brightly in a cloudless sky, the wind had picked up and tossed the long grass that poked up through the hard road surface. A slight chill gripped Vicky and ran gooseflesh up her arms. As she hugged herself tight, she clenched her jaw. "Life is change, Rhys. Without it, we'll stagnate and never improve our existence."

"I'll let Flynn go out when I think he's ready."

Her best friend in this world, Vicky had nothing but

compassion when she looked back at the man. "I think he's ready now. Besides, I'm not talking about Flynn anymore; I'm talking about me."

Rhys's face turned pale. He must have sensed Vicky's dissatisfaction with her life.

"I've been the spare part in your family dynamic for over a decade now."

Rhys shook his head and he frowned at her. "No. Think about what you're saying, Vicky."

"Look, I can't control when you choose to take your son out, but I can't wait forever either. Ten years is a long time to simply exist. I love you guys; you're more of a family than I've had in a long fucking time, but I need to move on."

"No."

Vicky tensed up when Rhys's voice echoed through the seemingly abandoned streets. After she'd looked at their surroundings, she glowered at him.

He lowered his voice. "No."

"I thought this nightmare would end eventually." Vicky sighed. "But it hasn't. The diseased outnumber us ten to one, twenty to one. Hell, they probably outnumber us ten thousand to one. Sure, many have died, but they're still the dominant species now. They're built to survive. If we're to stop them, we need to go to war with them. If we're to go to war with them, we need—"

"An army," Rhys said.

"Exactly!"

"And where will you get one of them from?"

As she scanned their surroundings, Vicky walked over to the

funnel they had set up. Much like the ones they had rigged up back at the containers, they'd tied it to an upright pole outside the petrol station. It made sense to have their water supply in a few separate places. They'd used a funnel to catch rainwater, and it had a bottle beneath it.

The bottle, although only a third full, would be enough. Vicky removed it and picked the lid up that they'd left beside it. She screwed the lid on, replaced the bottle with a spare one from her rucksack, and put the water in her bag. It had proven the most efficient way to collect water. Although thirsty, Vicky would wait until she'd boiled it later. Who knew what floated in the air nowadays? Better to wait a while longer than to take any risks.

When she looked up at Rhys, Vicky found him staring straight at her. "So?"

She shrugged. "So what?"

"Where will you go?"

With her bag still off her shoulders, Vicky removed the wind-up radio.

Rhys's eyes widened to see the small plastic device. "Where did you get *that* from?"

"I found it weeks ago."

"Why didn't you tell me about it?"

"I needed time to think."

"About?"

Another look around and Vicky couldn't see any diseased, so she wound the small black handle on the back of the radio. When she let it go, the message from the day before played out.

"Home is a place ..."

Vicky waited for Rhys to speak after the message had finished.

"How do you know it's legit?" Rhys finally said.

"It changes every few weeks, so someone's controlling it."

"But how do you know this is the paradise they promise?"

"I don't."

"And you're prepared to take that risk?"

"Rhys," Vicky said, "I've stagnated for ten years now. *Ten* years! That's a long time to do nothing for. At this point, I don't care if it's a trap or not. Hell, I'm living in a fucking prison in my container anyway. It's time for a change."

Moisture glistened in Rhys' eyes. "But what about us? What will *we* do?"

"This is why I keep talking about Flynn going out with you."

Although he looked like he wanted to argue, Rhys dipped his head and looked at the ground. After he'd released a heavy sigh, he said, "Okay. I understand."

When he looked back up again, Vicky watched the sadness leave his face and his attention flick to over her shoulder.

After a decade of scavenging with Rhys, Vicky knew that look all too well. A second later, the roar of the diseased lifted the hairs on the back of her neck.

Chapter Nine

Just one diseased, it had its mouth spread wide as it focused on them through the dried and bloody pits that were once its eyes. The creature came at them with the speed of an Olympic sprinter. It waved its arms in front of it as if to reach out to them. Its awkward gait did nothing to slow it down.

Vicky snapped her telescopic baton to full length with a *crack*. Although she'd done this thousands of times, her pulse raced to the edge of panic and a line of sweat lifted beneath her collar. One bad judgment and it would be game over.

When the diseased got to within three strides of the pair, Vicky jumped to the side and brought the baton up and around the side of the creature's head. Its face snapped to one side, and a wet *pop* sounded as blood sprayed away from it. Vicky had gotten so used to her weapon, she could knock the wings off a fly in flight with it. She'd also learned to go for the chin. A knockout proved to be the safest blow.

As she'd expected, the creature continued forward with its momentum before it crashed, face first, into one of the forecourt's petrol pumps.

A loud *boom* sounded out as it bounced off the pump and fell limp. Two of the hoses fell from their holders and clattered as they landed on top of it.

Vicky loomed over the creature, now just a tangle of limbs and rubber pipes, and delivered a second blow. With a sharp whack to the temple, the balled end of her baton sank into the thing's cranium and put the fucker's lights out.

When Vicky looked up at Rhys, he gave her a gentle nod. They had an agreement—three or less and they'd stay to fight them. It made much more sense than running, and if they could contribute in some way to the eradication of a few more diseased, then they'd done some good at least.

Rhys had started counting his kills until Vicky told him he sounded like Legolas from *Lord of the Rings*. He shut the fuck up after that—especially when she added that he looked nothing like the elven Adonis.

Before either of them could speak, the familiar cry of the diseased cut to Vicky's core. A chill ran through her as she looked in the direction of the sound. However many ran toward them at that moment, they numbered far more than three.

Rhys, who stood closer to the alleyway that led back to the field, took off, and Vicky ran after him.

As Vicky moved, she folded her baton, slipped it into her pocket, and watched Rhys vault the stile. When she got there a few seconds later, she glanced behind to see at least fifteen of the horrible fuckers, their faces strained from how fast they ran. Regardless of how often she'd seen it, Vicky would never get used to the determination with which they gave chase. Nothing mattered more to them than live human flesh.

Like Rhys had done, Vicky jumped over the stile. Her partner had a good twenty-metre lead on her, but she could see him. As long as he stayed ahead, she only needed to worry about herself.

As Vicky burst out into the field, she looked behind again to see the diseased funnel into the alleyway. No matter how many chased them, the two stiles and tight space always slowed them down.

By the time the containers came into view, Vicky's lungs burned and her head spun. She saw Flynn stand on his tiptoes and look down at his father, and then Vicky. His deep voice called out, "Mum."

Although Vicky couldn't see Larissa, it only took a few seconds for the *boom* of the weight against the shipping container. The diseased on the other side of the tree line—the ones in the airport—screamed and all rushed forward.

After a particularly good haul, Vicky and Rhys had taken a week off. In that time, most of the diseased had vanished from the airport. Although, the second they went out again, the horrible creatures returned in force. It seemed that no matter how long they left it, the diseased were always ready to reappear in vast numbers.

With time to spare, Vicky jumped onto the bottom of the ladder and scurried up to the top of the container to join Rhys.

Always one to wear his heart on his sleeve, Flynn gripped Vicky in a tight hug. "Thank God you're okay. Well done on another good run. Well done."

When Flynn let go of her, Vicky forced a smile at him. Would he be as happy when he heard what she had to say? Because this could be one of the last hugs she might ever get from him, Vicky grabbed him again and squeezed.

Chapter Ten

They could only do so much with water and vegetables, but at least they had food. The small allotment they'd made near the shipping containers had provided enough to keep them going for the time they'd been there. In the early days, they'd surrounded the patch of churned earth with cars to box it in. Somehow it had been enough to keep the diseased out and had allowed them to work the land for the past decade. Vicky often looked at the rusty shells that surrounded their food source with an eye to replacing them. All that corrosion had to have an impact on their food. But, like most things in this world, something more pressing always came up.

The scavenging added flavour and excitement to the allotment food, but with the last of their supplies running out, it had been a barren few days. Vicky tilted her bowl to get the remainder of the plain broth, spooned a lump of potato into her mouth, and placed the bowl down on the floor of the brightly decorated container.

They had so many spare containers, they used one as the kitchen and one as a communal space to eat and hang out in.

When they'd first settled there, they tried to have the kitchen and dining area in the same place, but the smoke got too thick from cooking that they couldn't enjoy a meal in the tight space afterwards.

As the last to finish, Flynn ate his final mouthful of vegetable broth and got to his feet. Vicky and the others handed him their bowls and the boy stacked them before he climbed the ladder out of the container. As the one person who couldn't leave the containers, he'd been the kitchen hand for a few years now. At about age fourteen, they decided he should cook and clean as his way of contributing. Despite Vicky's previous perception of teenagers, the boy did it without complaint.

After she'd watched Flynn leave the container, Vicky looked down at the floor. Now that she'd finally told Rhys of her plans, her leaving felt more real than it ever had.

When Vicky lifted her head and looked around the container, she stared at the orange walls with their crudely painted pyramids. The colour and the act of painting the containers had been what kept them all on the right side of sanity; not to mention the exercise container, and the one they'd rigged up as a bathroom. They had a jug to catch rainwater and although they drank most of it, they also used it to shower with. The triad of creativity, physical health, and personal hygiene seemed to be the reason none of them had lost the plot so far.

Vicky laughed to herself and both Larissa and Rhys looked at her. "Do you remember the first night here?"

"Of course," Larissa said.

Rhys nodded.

As Vicky listened to the banging of the diseased against the steel walls, she shook her head. "I thought the noise would drive me insane. It felt like torture that was never going to end."

"It still drives me nuts," Larissa said. "At night mostly, when I can't sleep and have to listen to those *arseholes* outside. I feel like we got shafted. In most zombie films, the dead die out after a few months."

"But these aren't dead, are they?" Rhys said with a flat tone. "They're infected, but none of them have died yet. Well, plenty of them have died, but the virus isn't fatal."

Vicky watched Larissa look at Rhys for a few seconds before she tilted her head to one side. "What's going on, Rhys?" she said. "You seem sad. What's happened?"

The sound of panic rode Larissa's words, and who could blame her? They walked a tightrope over a world of madness, and at any point they could slip and fall. Before Rhys could reply, Vicky cleared her throat. "It's time, Larissa."

Larissa froze and her eyes widened. She shook her head. "No. No. No."

"Come on, Larissa, you knew this time would come. I can't stay here forever. A decade is more than long enough. I should have gone after the first few months, but Flynn was too young then."

"But it's safe here," Larissa said, her voice echoing in the tight space.

Speaking in a whisper to try to encourage the others to do the same, Vicky said, "Look, I get why you guys want to stay here. You have your boy in a safe situation, and who wouldn't want that for their kid? But I can't stay living the same day again and again. Wake up, go out for supplies, eat shitty broth—

maybe a rabbit if I'm lucky—go to bed." Vicky knocked against the side of her head when she said, "It's driving me *insane.*"

Before Larissa could respond, Rhys said, "She has a wind-up radio. She's found a broadcast from another community, and she thinks she should go there."

"I *am* going there, Rhys. They've changed the broadcast several times since I've been listening to it. There are other people out there. I have to go and check out who they are."

With her hand outstretched, Larissa said, "Let me hear it."

A glance up at the hole in the roof of the container and Vicky shook her head. "No. Not yet. I want us to celebrate Flynn's sixteenth birthday before I tell him. I want to see that little boy become a man first."

Although Larissa didn't speak again, she dropped her head in defeat.

"Flynn's old enough now," Rhys said. "I thought we could give him a sixteenth birthday party tomorrow to celebrate him becoming a man, and then tell him. Vicky caught a rabbit today; we can cook that for him tomorrow. Vicky needs to move on, and we need to prepare our son to have a future. He needs to learn how to survive in this world. We can still do supply runs if one of us stays back at the containers. Flynn and I can go out, and you can ready the ladders."

Larissa kept her head bowed, stared down at her lap, and didn't respond.

Chapter Eleven

The warmth of the sun pressed into Vicky's skin as she sat atop the shipping container with Larissa and Flynn. Now she had to live without the comforts of her old life, Vicky felt every change in season. Although over ten years had passed, she often craved the luxury of a centrally heated house, hot water, a working kettle, and food whenever she wanted it. So when the seasons changed, especially when the country heated up again, she breathed in every second of it.

When Vicky leaned back in her seat, the flimsy white plastic chair bowed beneath her weight. They'd brought the cheap garden furniture back to the containers because it had been easy to carry. Besides, the plastic shit only came out when they wanted to sit on top of the containers rather than in them.

"Happy birthday again," Larissa said as Vicky watched her pat her boy's shoulder.

Playing the archetypal teenager, Flynn shrugged the attention off. "We don't *know* if it's my actual birthday or not today. We barely know what month it is. We could even be wrong on the year."

"What does it matter?" Vicky asked. "That makes today as good a day as any to have your birthday, doesn't it?"

Flynn shrugged, always more willing to listen to Vicky than his parents. "Yeah, I s'pose so."

Silence descended on the three and Vicky looked out at the diseased below. To eat on top of one of the containers could be seen as provocative. Their presence seemed to stir up something in the mob, which had gotten louder and far more agitated since they'd moved up top. The fuckers bashed into the containers, and a constant *boom* of bodies against steel sounded out.

A shake of her head and Vicky looked at Flynn and Larissa. "I don't know how you two put up with the sound all the time. One of the best things about going on supply runs is that I get away from their constant banging."

"Maybe it makes it worse," Larissa said.

"Huh?"

"Well, it's an ever-present noise for us, so we learn to deal with it. I can imagine getting away from it would make it seem worse when you return."

As she paused to listen to the groans and thuds, Vicky shrugged. "Yeah, maybe you're right." She hooked her thumb in the direction of the main mob. "Although, I can't imagine *ever* getting used to that."

At that moment, Rhys emerged from the kitchen container carrying a steaming pot.

With raised eyebrows, Flynn looked over at his dad. "What's in the pot?"

"Stew," Rhys said, and Flynn physically deflated. A twinkle lit in Rhys's eyes. "*Rabbit* stew."

Flynn gasped so sharp, it called out over the heads of the gathered diseased. Vicky looked out across the airport as if to watch the sound run away from them. She looked at the open patches of the runway that would have been taken up with diseased a few years back. Soon there'd be so much grass pushing up through the asphalt that they'd not see any at all. Before long, nature would grow through the buildings until places like London and New York looked like the ruined temples of Angkor Wat.

When Rhys placed the steaming bowl of stew in front of her, Vicky picked up her spoon and tucked in. As she chewed on the rich meat, she closed her eyes, tasted its strong flavour, and drew a deep breath. They didn't get meat anywhere near as much as she would have liked.

***

Once they'd finished their stew, Rhys cleared his throat to get everyone's attention. A few diseased down below roared louder for the noise, and Rhys leaned back to shout at them, "Shut up, you noisy bastards."

Flynn smirked.

"Flynn, my boy." Rhys took a heavy breath as if to prevent himself from crying. "When the world went to shit, I had nothing but your survival on my mind." When he looked at Larissa and Vicky, he smiled. "We all did. I remember feeling safe when we realised we could live in these containers. But for a long time I've thought 'and then what?'. I mean, we've survived, right? We *are* surviving, but there has to be something more."

The words resonated with Vicky, but she refrained from adding to the conversation. Best to let Rhys talk to his boy.

"Well, that day has come for us to find something more. You're a man now, son. You've grown up to be strong, brave, and emotionally well-balanced. Hell, maybe every kid needs two mums and one dad to turn them into the wonderful person you've become."

As Vicky watched Larissa cry, she swallowed back the lump in her throat and blinked against the itch of tears. Regardless of what Rhys said at that moment, she had to move on. She'd thought about it for years now, and had purposefully waited until this time. It didn't matter how much she loved the three of them. It didn't matter that she thought of Flynn like a son.

"What I'm trying to say is," Rhys said, "I'm going to take you out foraging with me." When he looked at the field behind the container, Rhys said, "At first we'll just get you farming down there in the allotment, but as you learn to cope with the diseased on the ground, we'll go farther and farther out."

Vicky leaned across and grabbed Flynn's thick arm. "It'll do you good to learn how to survive in this world."

Flynn stared at Vicky and his eyes narrowed. "There's something else, isn't there?"

A glance at Rhys and Larissa, and Vicky looked back at the boy. After a gulp of hot air, she said, "Come on, Flynn, surely you knew this day would come?"

"You're *leaving*?"

The accusation in his tone cut to Vicky's core. No matter how she looked at it, by leaving the shipping containers, she was leaving him.

Flynn's voice became shrill, which raised the level of agitation down below. "How can you do this to us? How can you *leave*?"

"Flynn," Vicky reached across to touch him again but he pulled his arm away. "I've been waiting for you to get old enough so I could move on. I love you all very much, but I *need* something more. I believe there are other people out there. I'm *lonely*, Flynn."

"I'm sure there's not anyone else out there. Don't you think we would have seen some of these people by now if there were?"

Without another word, Vicky pulled her wind-up radio from her pocket.

"What's that?" Flynn said.

The wheel clicked as Vicky wound it. Once she'd twisted it around several full rotations, she let go and the message played.

"*...our vision. Home is located just near Britnall. The ...*"

Vicky turned the radio off once the message had played in its entirety.

"How do you know it's real?" Flynn asked, his wide eyes still on the radio.

"Because they change it every few weeks. Someone is still taking the time to update this message, so I have to go out and find who it is."

"It could be a trap."

"It could be."

"That's it?" Flynn asked. "I don't want you to walk into a trap."

"No, Flynn, neither do I, but I'm at the point where I'm prepared to take the risk. I *have* to see what this is. I have to find out."

Although still clearly upset, Flynn didn't have anything else for Vicky. A deep scowl hooded his eyes, and he sat with his jaw clenched tight.

Vicky reached into her jacket pocket and pulled out something wrapped in a carrier bag. She handed it to the boy.

"What's this?"

"Your birthday present."

A shake ran through Flynn's hands as she opened the package. "This has got to be the first year that you haven't given me schoolbooks."

"Schoolbooks are important."

The wrapping didn't hide what the gift was, and when Vicky looked up at Rhys and Larissa, she could see the shock on both of their faces.

"Your catapult?" Flynn said as he stared down at the object in his hands. "I can't take this from you. What will you do?"

"I want you to have it. I can still hunt with a spear, or a baseball bat; I'll be all right."

Grief buckled Flynn's bottom lip as he turned the well-worn catapult over in his hands and stared down at it. A warble shook his words. "Just promise me one thing." When he looked up, tears glistened in his eyes.

"Okay," Vicky said.

Flynn's entire face twisted with his sadness. "If you get the chance to, come back and see us."

Vicky smiled through her grief and reached across to touch Flynn's forearm. "Of *course* I will." She looked at Rhys and Larissa to see both of them were crying, and she made the promise to them too. "Of course I will."

Chapter Twelve

Vicky wiped the rainwater from her eyes. Not that it did her any good. The rain lashed down and made it hard to see regardless of what she did—fuck knows how they'd hear the diseased approaching.

"Should we be out in this?" Flynn asked as he hopped over the stile after his dad.

A glance behind her just to be sure, and Vicky followed the pair of them over to the road on the other side.

"It's not ideal," Rhys said, "but Vicky's waited for a decade now, and it's time to let her move on."

There could have been judgement in his voice. After all, he didn't hide the fact that Vicky's moving on hurt him, but instead, he spoke with compassion. A true friend. Rhys may not have said it, but his actions showed that he appreciated how she'd done right by him and his family. In another time with another set of circumstances, maybe Vicky and Rhys could have made a go of it.

As they walked across the road, tufts of grass pushing up through the hard asphalt, Vicky watched Flynn. The boy looked around with wide eyes, his jaw loose as he took everything in. Rhys had initially said they'd take him to the allotment and back, but Vicky had agreed to go on one last supply run. They could give Flynn a better experience while they both looked out for him.

The gate to the next field had been knocked down five years previously when Vicky and Rhys had grown tired of climbing the wobbly thing. The field beyond it had long grass like all of the other fields that surrounded the airport. A flattened path ran through the middle of it, trodden down over the years by Vicky and Rhys.

As they walked, Vicky held the whistle around her neck. Probably not a good idea to use a whistle when the diseased responded to sound in the way they did, but Larissa needed to do the job of two people now, and it had seemed like the best plan. Not only did she need to bang against the container, but she also needed to lower the ladder to let them up when they got back. Because she couldn't do both at the same time, she needed to know when to abandon one for the other.

The grass along the side of the stream also lay flat from where Vicky and Rhys had pushed it down. With nets set up to catch fish, they needed the grass flattened to give them the manoeuvrability to pull them in. Not the most advanced way to fish. The keep nets they'd set up on the side of the stream did the job though. About once a week they'd catch at least something, which was far better than nothing.

"This is where the fish come from," Rhys said to his son.

Vicky stood back to remove herself from the father and son bonding. She would be out of the picture soon, so the less she intervened, the better.

After he'd edged slightly closer to the water, Flynn peered in. "What, the fish just swim in?"

"Yeah, we have the top of the net high up, so when they swim in, they can't get out again."

As Flynn edged another step closer, Vicky watched the long grass around them for signs of the diseased. The strong wind threw the rain at her so hard it stung, and it tossed the grass from side to side. Anything could be lurking nearby, and they wouldn't have a hope of seeing it. Before Vicky could suggest they moved, she looked back at the father and son.

Rhys smiled at his boy. A man deprived of a conventional existence, Vicky had to let them be normal for once. It didn't always have to be about surviving. Maybe today, it could just be about fishing.

A rock of anxiety twisted Vicky's guts as she continued to look around. As much as she tried to tap into her other senses, the heavy rain deadened them all. Sound, smell, sight ….

Vicky watched Flynn take another step closer to the water. When she saw it, she inhaled to call out and reached for the boy, but before she could let out a sound, he'd already slipped. Everything slowed down. Although not very deep, the stream ran deep enough for a boy who couldn't swim.

But before he fell in, Rhys sprung to life, caught him, and pulled him away. As he dragged his son from the water and pushed him into the long grass, he fell in himself. The splash seemed to stop time for a moment, and Vicky froze.

When she looked to the left, she saw the grass move like it hadn't before. It had nothing to do with the wind. Before the diseased appeared, Vicky lurched forward, grabbed Flynn, and pulled him away.

Flynn screamed so loud it hurt Vicky's ears, and he resisted her as he watched the monsters pile into the water on top of his dad. Vicky quickly overpowered Flynn and dragged him back as several more diseased crashed into Rhys in the water. In that moment, Vicky made eye contact with the man she'd known so well for ten years, and she saw the defeat in his wide stare. She had but one job now; get Flynn back to safety.

After she'd pulled Flynn around in front of her, Vicky shoved him in the back toward the road. "Go, now! We need to get back to the container. Run, Flynn, and don't look back."

Flynn, clumsy with grief, ran with everything he had. Despite his clear struggle, he still moved like the wind and left Vicky behind.

A glance over her shoulder and Vicky watched the pile of diseased in the water. Rhys had already stopped fighting, and the water had turned red. He'd be one of them soon.

The grass, although flattened, still whipped at Vicky's legs as she ran after Flynn. With zero caution, she burst out into the road and followed the boy over the stile.

At the end of the alleyway, her heart pounding and her head spinning, Vicky caught up with Flynn.

The *boom* called out as Larissa hit the container with the weight.

"Follow the path I take," Vicky said to Flynn as she overtook him. "The field is uneven, so you need to watch where I step."

Vicky then lifted the whistle to her lips and blew hard. The high-pitched *peep* put a stop to the beat against the container from where Larissa had obviously heard them.

Although she looked behind, Vicky didn't see any diseased

on their tail. Larissa best be waiting for them anyway.

Just to be sure, she blew on the whistle again. With the rain as it was, she had to be certain Larissa had heard them.

As she pushed on, the boy close behind, Vicky looked out across the field and saw them. To their right, a mob of diseased about fifty strong came at them like a pack of wild horses. They looked like they could reach the containers before Vicky and Flynn did.

"Come on, Flynn," Vicky called to him as she fought for breath, "we need to hurry the fuck up."

Chapter Thirteen

Although the banging had stopped, when Vicky rounded the corner and looked up to where Flynn used to stand, she didn't see Larissa. A glance back at the red-faced Flynn and she looked back up at the container. "Come *on*, Larissa, speed it up."

The cries and yells from the pack of diseased to their right grew louder the closer they got. The diseased had different calls for different occasions; some of discontent, some of pain, some when they didn't even know you were there—the idle moaning and groaning of what sounded like perpetual torment. Then they had the calls that she heard now—the calls of excitement.

The whistle on the string around Vicky's neck slapped against her chest, and it took her three attempts to catch it as she ran. Gassed from the exertion, she pulled as large a breath as she could, and blew the whistle again.

This time, Larissa stood up on the container. Vicky should have felt relief, but she didn't because the whistle seemed to intensify the diseased's screams. Maybe they knew they'd now have to work harder for their prey. Instead of bursting to life, Vicky watched Larissa look down at her, Flynn, and then search behind them. Her entire frame sagged. The fear that one of them wouldn't return had always been there. No doubt Larissa had already worked out what Rhys's absence meant. But the lack of Rhys didn't matter at that moment.

Vicky pushed herself so hard her legs burned and her lungs felt just about ready to burst. She had a boy behind her to take care of, and a horde closing in from their right. Now she had to motivate Larissa to move too. A peer, and someone she'd learned to love like a sister, the sweet woman visibly broke as what must have been the realisation of her missing husband dawned on her. Even from the distance of at least fifty metres and through the heavy rain, Vicky watched Larissa physically sag.

Vicky turned to look at Flynn again. The boy seemed to have lost a bit of distance to her. Tears ran down his red cheeks, and his features twisted from the pain of the sprint. No matter how much the kid had trained before that day, until he'd run from a diseased, he couldn't prepare for it. Adrenaline could spur you on, but it could also rob you of your power. The boy seemed to be lagging, but they couldn't stop.

"Pick your pace up, Flynn," Vicky screamed at him. "If you don't hurry the fuck up, you'll be one of them soon."

As happened with every pack of diseased, a couple of front runners broke away from the rest. A woman, naked save for a pair of hot pants, had taken an early lead. Her small and dirty breasts shook with every step. Flynn needed to move quicker.

But Vicky couldn't wait for him. The boy had to grow into a man and be responsible for his own well-being. Instead, she sped up. Give him something to chase and hopefully, he'd rise to the challenge.

With Rhys's dying face in her mind, Vicky closed in on the containers and left the teenage boy behind.

When Vicky got to within a few metres, Larissa finally dropped the ladder down. Once she'd caught up to it, Vicky stood on the bottom rung. She'd climb it when she needed to, but if she could get Flynn up as well, then she would.

As the boy continued to push on, Vicky clapped her hands together and shouted so loud it hurt her throat. "That's it, Flynn. Keep it coming, you can do it."

The semi-naked woman had closed the gap between them to no more than a couple of metres at best. With her heart in her throat, Vicky looked up at Larissa to see the woman crying freely. "I'm going to save him," Vicky said. "Make sure you're ready to lift the ladder once we're both up."

It looked like a nod, but Vicky didn't have time to confirm it. As she ran at Flynn, she snapped her baton to its full length.

The woman behind the boy roared for all she had and lunged at him. Vicky caught her in the centre of her forehead with the balled end of the baton. The impact ran a sharp sting up Vicky's arm, drove the woman backwards, and threw her down hard on the ground. Flynn kept running at the ladder.

By the time Vicky had turned around and headed back for the containers, Flynn had jumped onto the ladder and had climbed halfway up it.

Although she didn't look back at the diseased, Vicky heard them. Hell, she felt their stampede beneath her feet. A second later and their collective smell hit her. The smell of this world, the culmination of a pack of diseased concentrated as a fetid blast.

When she got close to the bottom of the ladder, she caught the pack in her peripheral vision. With her entire body on fire from the effort of the run, she looked up at Larissa. "Be ready to pull this thing up."

Too busy comforting her son, Larissa didn't even look down at Vicky.

"*Larissa*! Pull the ladder up after me."

Nothing.

With a few steps left on the ladder and now only a few metres from Larissa, Vicky slipped the whistle into her mouth and blew hard.

Larissa jumped and looked at her.

"Pull the fucking ladder up before the diseased follow me."

Having got through to the woman, Vicky jumped up onto the container and landed hard on the steel surface with a loud *boom*. As she lay face down, she panted and gasped for breath while she listened to the sound of the ladder sliding against the container from where Larissa pulled it up.

Vicky rolled over onto her back in time to see Larissa drop the ladder onto the container with a *clang*. She then watched the woman fall to her knees and release a demented and broken wail. The hundreds of diseased that surrounded them joined in with her cries, their clear frustration at missing yet another meal.

Chapter Fourteen

Flynn may have sounded like a young man when he spoke, but when he screamed, he returned to the little boy Vicky had watched grow up over the past decade. The tone of his high-pitched cry, amplified by the metal container he lived in, woke Vicky from her restless sleep with a start. Had he been on his own, then she would have slept in with the boy, but he had his mother by his side, and though Vicky hurt over the loss of Rhys too, they needed to share their grief without her.

With the lethargy of sleep still deep in her muscles, Vicky sat up in her container as Flynn continued to cry. He sounded like an enraged primate, his screams coming in bellowed and furious waves. After she'd slipped her shoes on, she reached up for the ladder in her container and pulled herself to her feet. Still clumsy with tiredness, and with her eyes stinging, she dragged herself toward the daylight above.

The stench of shit and rot hit Vicky as soon as she poked her head out of the container. The diseased joined in with Flynn's cries, their agitation setting the air alight; their prey stood just metres away but they had no way of reaching it.

Atop the containers, Vicky looked over to where they usually dropped the ladder into the field behind the airport. It had been lowered. But if Flynn remained in his container …

Instead of going to the boy, Vicky ran for the ladder. Her footsteps boomed against the three containers she crossed to get to it. At the precise moment she peered down into the field, a pack of diseased came around the corner as if they'd gotten wind of a chance to get to them. Vicky gripped the cold aluminium ladder and yanked it up. A second later, the container shook beneath her feet from where the pack crashed into it.

Without taking her eyes off the mob below, Vicky dropped the ladder on top of the container with a loud *clang*.

Although they'd bridged the gaps over the containers with ladders, Vicky ignored them as she hopped from one to the other in the direction of Flynn's cries.

Still early enough for there to be low-lying fog on the airfield, the containers had a slight coating of dew, but not enough to encourage Vicky to slow down. She jumped another gap and looked at the diseased below as she crossed it. No matter how long she lived with them, the sight of the beasts still ran ice through her veins, especially on days like today when they seemed to be rising out of the fog.

In one fluid movement, Vicky jumped onto Flynn's ladder and climbed down into his container.

When she got to the bottom, she found the boy. His features were twisted with grief as tears ran down his face. He paced his small container, frantic in his disturbed state.

Vicky looked around the sleeping quarters, the walls a garish mix of lime green and turquoise, and shrugged. "Where's your mum?"

But Flynn didn't reply. He didn't seem to have it in him. Instead, he walked over and handed Vicky a scrap of paper. Larissa had written on it in pencil, and Vicky had to read it twice to be sure she'd taken the message in.

The air left her lungs when she looked back up at Flynn and whispered. "She's gone?"

Flynn pointed at the paper. "To find some supplies."

Vicky read the note for a third time.

Dear Flynn,

It's not fair that we expect Vicky to wait with us, so I'm going to go out and hunt for food. I'll be back soon, so please don't worry about me or follow me. I'll be fine. We've survived this long; we'll continue to survive.

I love you, little boy.

Love
Momma Bear xxx.

"Fuck," Vicky said. Without another word, she jumped on the ladder out of the container and shot up it. She crossed back to where she'd lifted the ladder up that led down into the field.

Flynn appeared at her side a few seconds later, and he too stared down at the angry faces below. The diseased all looked up at them, their mouths working as if they could taste the pair. Some of them had fur and blood around their mouths from where they'd clearly eaten something non-human.

A sharp grip dug into Vicky's bicep, and when she turned to look at Flynn, she saw his wide and bloodshot eyes stare out toward another pack of diseased who'd just come into view.

Maybe Vicky saw it before Flynn did, but maybe not. Regardless, the boy spoke it first as he looked at the diseased woman at the front of the pack. Fresh blood ran from the hole that had been bitten into her cheek, and her eyes bled waterfalls down her face. In her grip she had a bag with tins and bottled water in; the supplies she'd gone to fetch.

Flynn's legs gave way beneath him, and he hit the container with a loud *boom*. As he curled up in a ball, he rasped just one word… "Mum."

Chapter Fifteen

Day and night blended into one another; especially inside a shipping container, regardless of how brightly it had been painted. Vicky comforted Flynn as he grieved for the loss of both parents. She'd remained at his beck and call, and only rested when he did. Mostly, he cried until he collapsed with exhaustion, only to wake a few hours later to sob all over again.

About a week had passed since Flynn had last seen his mum in the field behind the airport. Fortunately, Vicky had had the foresight to ration their supplies since then. They'd stretched their food so thin that hunger now gnawed away at Vicky's concave stomach as if her starvation could eat her alive.

But she wasn't starving. She knew that. Just hungry. Fucking hungry! At some point, they would have to make a decision that involved getting more food. To do that, they would have to move on.

With Flynn asleep in his bed, Vicky left him in the container. She held her breath as she climbed his ladder. It did nothing to quiet the aluminium rungs that creaked beneath her weight.

Once up top, Vicky squinted against the daylight and crept across the containers to the end by the field where Larissa still waited for them. Unlike all of the other diseased, Larissa didn't leave. She just stood there. Vicky had watched her grow skinnier with each passing day; she looked ill—even for an infected.

Not that Vicky could see her irises, but she saw sadness on her face as she looked up. Almost like an addict that stared at the needle she both hated and craved. It seemed like she had some awareness of who Vicky was, but would still bite her in a heartbeat.

Maybe Larissa would fall down dead at the container if she waited for longer than her body could last without sustenance. Not that the diseased died easily; the virus seemed to give them a longevity that only required them to eat and drink occasionally.

A sudden distressed scream from Flynn snapped both Vicky and Larissa from the stare that locked them onto one another. Vicky burst to life and ran over the containers. "Don't worry, Flynn," she called out, the corrugated surface rolling and turning her ankles as she moved. "I've not gone anywhere. I'm coming."

As Vicky ran, the usual stirrings of discontent rose from the diseased below.

After she'd descended into the container, she found Flynn sat up in bed and crying. She hugged him close to her. The pair rocked together as Flynn sobbed into her shoulder. Flynn hadn't done much else for the past week. As she'd done since Larissa had gone, Vicky sat with him until he had no more tears to cry.

***

The look on Larissa's face had stayed with Vicky all night. Flynn had fallen asleep in her arms again, and she continued to hold him. Aches ran through her body as she gripped Flynn and leaned up against the cold wall of the metal container.

The vibration of the diseased as they crashed against the container shook through Vicky's back and served as a constant reminder that had been there for over a decade. As Vicky looked at the turquoise and lime-green walls, she saw a spot in the corner where an angry cross had been scratched into the paintwork. Unsure as to what it represented—other than a frantic obsession in the repeated marks—she looked down at Flynn's hand and saw the paint beneath his nails. He must have done it when she'd gone up top. They'd spent too much time in these cursed containers. They had to get out. There had to be something better than this.

***

When the early morning sun lifted to the point of lighting up the inside of the container, Flynn stirred in Vicky's arms. She loosened her hug to allow the boy to sit up straight. As he looked at her, he blinked several times. A confused frown crushed his face.

Vicky silently counted down from ten in her head. When she got to zero, Flynn hadn't cried yet. For the first time since his mum had gone, he hadn't cried after waking.

After a few minutes of silence, Flynn still held it together, so Vicky took the opportunity. "We need to move on soon, mate."

Nervous of his response, Vicky winced as she watched him. But he said nothing.

"We need to find somewhere other than this to live. We can't stay here anymore. I know this place reminds you of your mum and dad, and I'm sad to leave that behind too, but it won't work here with just two of us. It's going to be risky, so we may as well try to find Home. What do you think?"

Although he didn't speak, Flynn bit down on his bottom lip and nodded at Vicky. He saw the sense in it too.

A few seconds later, the light caught the tears in Flynn's eyes and his mouth bent out of shape. "I miss Mum and Dad, Vicky. I miss them so much."

"I know, mate," Vicky said as she held him close to her. She cleared the lump in her throat and blinked against the itch of tears forming in her eyes. "I know."

Chapter Sixteen

Sweat lifted along Vicky's brow as she stood over Flynn's container and peered in. A hot day to move on, but now that they'd decided to go, they needed to follow through with it.

Vicky watched Flynn slowly move around down below, his small rucksack bulging with all the things he wanted to take. The first two things he'd gone for when they decided to leave were Rhys's hat that he always wore, and Larissa's bracelet. She'd taken it off before she went on her supply run for some reason. Maybe she knew she'd never come back. After Vicky cleared the lump in her throat, she called down to Flynn, a warble in her voice. "Come on, mate, we need to go."

But Flynn ignored her; he clearly needed a little longer. And she got it, she really did; the container had been all the boy had known for the past decade. The hardest part would be to walk away from it. In an unstable world, those seventeen shitty shipping containers had given him some kind of consistency.

Although she wanted to call down to him again, Vicky walked over to the edge of the container that led to the field behind the airport. To look at Larissa got no easier with repetition. The woman she'd known so well had gone; Vicky barely recognised the thing that stared back at her now. In one slow movement, Larissa opened her jaw to reveal a blackness inside her pit of a mouth, and she released a long hiss. The sadness that Vicky thought she'd seen in Larissa's eyes had well and truly left her now. The thing wandering below didn't even hold the memory of Larissa. Another diseased, it now stood free of personality. Just another member of the hive mind.

A chill snaked through Vicky's body, so she turned away from Larissa and walked back over to Flynn.

"Come on," she said as she crossed back over the couple of containers. But before she could peer down into his again, Flynn poked his head above the surface.

Vicky stopped and watched him climb out. He pulled his shoulders back as if to adjust his rucksack and stared at Vicky before he said, "You need to be more patient."

As she looked out over the fields behind the airport, the town of Biggin Hill beyond it, Vicky shrugged. "I want to make the most of the daylight. I dunno about you, but I want to arrive at Home as soon as possible."

"See, that's what this is all about, isn't it?"

Before Vicky could reply, Flynn continued. "It's all about you getting your way. And now you don't have to go to Home on your own, it's worked out nicely. That's what you wanted, wasn't it?"

Flynn's words drove a spear into Vicky's heart and her vision blurred. The accusation with which he stared at her cut straight to her core. Not many people in this life had that power over her, but he had her heart.

Flynn remained still and continued to stare at her. Vicky could have ignored his accusation—and she nearly did—but it would come up again at some point. Better now than when they were in the thick of it. After a deep breath, she blinked repeatedly and said, "Yes, Flynn, I wanted to go to Home, and I would have loved for you all to come with me." Her voice broke because of the lump in her throat. "But *not* like this."

She shook her head. "Not like this at all."

***

The moment passed, and Flynn didn't say anything else about it. Instead, he turned his back on Vicky and ground his jaw. After a few minutes, Vicky grabbed his arm.

Flynn spun around and stared at her.

"Just wait there, okay?" she said.

With a scowl so hard it hooded his eyes, Flynn glared at Vicky.

"Please?"

Although Flynn didn't reply, he remained still.

Vicky jumped the gaps between a couple of containers and arrived at the place where they banged the heavy weight down.

A dent sat in the steel from years of being bashed. Like a church bell calling to the congregation, it rang out every time Vicky and Rhys had left the containers, and every time they came back again. Haunting, but it provided some kind of reassurance to Vicky when she heard it. It told her that no matter how many of the fuckers chased her, she wasn't on her own. A tight team, the four of them could cope with anything—at least, that's what she thought.

Weak with grief, Vicky lifted the weight and let it fall against the top of the container with a resounding *boom*. Vicky then lifted and dropped it again. It hit a slightly different spot and returned a different tone, higher in pitch than the one before it.

As she found her flow, Vicky watched the diseased below walk toward the container. After every knock, more of them appeared as though it were a never-ending stream of horror and rot.

***

By the time Larissa had joined the other diseased on the airport runway, Vicky's arms ached and sweat ran into her stinging eyes. It had taken about ten minutes for the woman to find her way around.

So hot, Vicky nearly removed her sweatshirt. But she needed it with her, and to wear it would be the easiest way to carry it. She needed to be ready to leave in a heartbeat.

Larissa nudged and shuffled her way through the crowd until she got to directly below Vicky. The blood in her eyes had dried, yet she—like all of them—stared up as if she could still see. And to judge them by the way they moved with intent, they *could* still see. Maybe the blood put a red lens across their vision, an enraged tint to everything they saw.

Confident Larissa would remain where she stood, Vicky continued to beat against the container and looked over at Flynn. "Lower the ladder now, mate. Get ready and I'll come and join you."

With her attention on the boy, Vicky beat her booming call. She watched him lower the ladder to the ground and remain on top of the container. Despite his size, the scared little boy looked over the edge like he always had. He'd have to grow up fast to survive, and she'd probably have to drag him every step of the way.

If only Rhys and Larissa had forced him to grow up sooner as she'd suggested.

With her shoulders burning from the effort, Vicky stopped banging the weight against the container and stood up with it still in her hands. She stared down at the diseased and watched as they screamed and hissed at her.

As she lifted the weight above her head, she focused on Larissa. Were the roles reversed, Vicky wouldn't want to exist as one of them. No fucking way.

Vicky screamed as she threw the heavy weight down. On its way to the ground, the weight smashed into Larissa's face. The metal lump sank into her nose with a *crack,* and it knocked Larissa back.

The diseased parted and looked down at one of their own, dead on the ground. As one, they returned their attention to Vicky and screamed louder than before.

Vicky bit down on her bottom lip and flipped them the bird before she spun on her heel and jogged across the containers that separated her from Flynn.

Without missing a beat, Vicky arrived on Flynn's container, grabbed the top of the ladder, and climbed down it. When she reached the ground, she looked back up to see Flynn hesitate. "Come on, mate, we need to get the fuck out of here."

The groans and moans of the diseased called around the container at her. They hadn't worked out where she'd gone yet, but it wouldn't be long.

Just before she could shout at the boy again, he started his descent.

As he climbed down, Vicky checked around them. The coast seemed clear so far.

When the boy reached the ground, Vicky grabbed both of his hands in hers. "Okay, this is it now. I need you to follow me and run like the wind, all right?"

Flynn nodded.

When Vicky took off, Flynn followed behind. For the first time since they'd been at the containers, they left the ladder down. The diseased didn't seem able to climb, but let them try now. Hopefully a few of them would fall into the containers, and it would give the world a couple less to deal with.

The sun's heat hit the back of Vicky's head as she ran, and the sound of Flynn's footsteps chased behind her. Thankfully, Flynn's were the only footsteps she heard.

… for now.

Chapter Seventeen

Vicky hadn't said much to Flynn for the past hour or so, and he hadn't tried to speak either. As she scanned their surroundings, on high alert for what could jump out on them at any moment, she caught sight of Flynn doing the same.

When they reached an old high street, Flynn stopped in his tracks and Vicky pulled up next to him. A strong wind tore down the deserted thoroughfare and cut straight to Vicky's core. Vicky looked at Flynn to see him continue to scan the street, his eyes wide, his head movements twitchy.

"It's a good idea to stop every once in a while," she said. "It may look clear, but if you're going to survive out here, you need to be extra vigilant. Well done."

Like everywhere else, grass grew up through the cracks in the road. Smashed shop windows and signs hanging from posts swung in the wind. Old cars had rusted where they sat, their tyres flat.

Flynn still didn't seem keen on moving off, so Vicky said, "What's up?"

"I think we should go around."

"Go around where?"

"I dunno," Flynn shrugged, "just get off the high street maybe? It just doesn't feel right out here."

"Your dad and I picked this area clean for the past decade. What we learned very quickly was that high streets are no more dangerous than residential areas. Despite what George A. Romero has told us—"

"Who?" Flynn interrupted.

"An old movie director. He made zombie films that showed hordes of the fuckers turning up to shopping malls. He made it look like visiting the places was in their DNA. I remember Rhys laughing every time we entered a diseased-free shop. The diseased couldn't give two shits about commerce. They care about food; that's all. You're as likely to find them skulking around fields hunting rabbits as you are to find them in built up areas snacking on rats."

Wide-eyed, Flynn chewed on his bottom lip as he watched their surroundings. "At least you'd see them more easily in fields."

"That's true, but to avoid the built up areas around here will take us on a huge detour. We'll be exposed for much longer just because of the extra time it will take to get to Home. The risk isn't worth it." A yellowed piece of newspaper skittered across the road between them. "We just need to have our wits about us and keep on going. The quickest way to Home is straight through this town." Looking up at the strong sun, Vicky said, "We have quite a few hours of daylight left, so let's make the most of the light and get through the town."

The snap of Vicky's telescopic baton echoed off the shop

fronts on either side of the street, and she walked with a slightly lowered stance; ready to kick off in a flash. Flynn followed her.

When Vicky heard a rustle, she spun around to find Flynn had stopped to retrieve the catapult she'd given him as a birthday present. The boy had it wrapped in a carrier bag.

Vicky reached up behind her head and grabbed the handle of her baseball bat. She had it wedged between her back and rucksack. After she'd pulled it free, she rolled her shoulders, relieved to finally remove the thing. She then handed it to Flynn. "Here, take this. A catapult won't do much for you here. If something comes at you, you won't have time to aim. You need to swing for the fucker to take it down."

After Flynn had tucked the catapult into the back of his trousers, he took the baseball bat, turned it over in his hands, and gulped.

Of all the shop signs on the high street, just one remained above its shop. Browned with age, the sign clearly used to be white. It had flourishing and joined-up purple writing on it. Vicky squinted as she stared at it for a few seconds before she worked out what it said. *Deja Vu*. A row of ripped leather chairs ran down either side of the shop. The once tiled floor had lost its battle against the grass that pushed up through it.

The slap of clumsy footsteps startled Vicky and she straightened where she stood. With the echoes created by the surrounding buildings, it took her a few seconds to pinpoint the sound. Just as she did, a diseased burst from an alleyway.

"What do we do, Vicky?" Flynn asked, his voice breathless and high in pitch.

As the thing closed down on them, pure hate on its face,

Vicky stepped aside. "*You* need to take it down."

Flynn gripped his bat with both hands and held it up, ready to swing. "Come *on*, Vicky, you can't be serious. I've never had to fight one of these things."

With one eye on the monster, Vicky said, "And no better time to start."

"Vicky?"

"Flynn, you have to learn to fight them. I can't carry both of us."

"Please, Vicky."

Tears ran down Flynn's face, but she couldn't step in. "You have to learn, Flynn. It's either kill or be killed; those are the options." While she gave him his ultimatum, Vicky stepped back a pace so the diseased would head for Flynn. The urge to protect him burned bright inside of her, but she held her ground. She thought of the kid like she would her own son, but this had to work. He'd do it. When the chips were down, he'd find it in him.

After she'd stepped back another pace, Vicky's mouth dried and her heart raced. Had she made the right call? He might not be ready. But he had to be ready. He had to try. With a bat and just one diseased, they had the perfect opportunity to practice.

"Get ready to swing for it, Flynn."

The boy wrung his grip on the bat and frowned against his tears.

"On the count of three," Vicky called as the diseased closed the gap.

"Three."

"Two."

The boy swung too early, and Vicky's heart leapt into her throat. The end of his bat just caught the diseased on the nose. It may have only skimmed it, but it made enough contact to knock its face to the side and to send the monster sprawling.

Flynn froze as he stared down at the thing with a look of horror. His chest rose and fell with his rapid breaths.

Only dazed, the diseased fought against its own lack of coordination as it tried to get up. Before it could fully right itself, Vicky rushed over to it and brought her baton down on the top of its head.

One hard whack later and Vicky had caved in the thing's skull. Blood pooled on the ground beneath it from where its soft brain had spilled from its broken cranium. The copper reek of blood surrounded Vicky, and the start of a heave sat in her throat.

With her hands on her hips, Vicky recovered her breath and looked down at the thing like she expected it to move. Not that she'd ever seen one of them recover from a brain injury, but then she'd never seen crazed infected lunatics before, so who knew what would happen next.

When Vicky turned to Flynn, she saw him standing in a state of shock. After she'd wiped the end of her baton on the diseased's clothes, she walked past Flynn on her way back up the high street. She patted his shoulder as she passed him. "You're a man now, Flynn; you need to learn to fight like one. The first is always the hardest, and you're still alive, so I'm not worried for you. It's going to be a steep learning curve, but you're ready for it."

Once Vicky had passed him, she released the longest sigh.

The anxiety of what she'd just put the boy through had wound so tight in her stomach it gave her indigestion. A glance behind and she saw Flynn remained rooted to the spot, so she called, "Come on, mate, we need to get the fuck out of here before more show up."

With one last look at the downed diseased, Flynn came to life and followed after Vicky.

Chapter Eighteen

"I did it, didn't I, Vicky?"

When Vicky looked across at Flynn, she couldn't help but smile at his temporary joy. To see the burden removed from his heavy shoulders, if just for a short while, lifted her spirit. "You did it, mate." Her smile widened as she continued to climb the steep hill. "You knocked your first diseased to the floor. That's the hardest kill, you know?"

Wide eyes stared back at her. "It is?"

It obviously hadn't registered the last time she'd said it to him. "Sure! Now you've done it once; you'll feel that little bit more confident to do it again. You'll knock plenty of the fuckers down before you reach the end of your life. Hell, you'll probably knock plenty of the fuckers down before you reach the end of the week."

Another smile, although crooked and slightly broken, lifted on Flynn's face. A life on top of the containers must have turned the terrifying world beyond into a truly hellish prospect. Flynn had done well so far to manage what must have been damn near crippling anxiety. Vicky needed to make sure killing the diseased became second nature to him. With both of his parents gone, she couldn't let Flynn die too. Now his nurturing—and survival—rested purely on her shoulders. With such a daunting task, she now saw why Rhys had stalled so much when she'd pushed him to let the boy grow up.

They walked up what used to be a main road, the incline steep enough to send a slight ache through Vicky's calf muscles. Nature pushed up through the hard surface and ran cracks all across it. A road between towns, hopefully there would be less diseased out here. Not that Vicky would ever lower her guard.

A rumble turned through Vicky's stomach so loud that Flynn heard it, even above the strong wind that swayed the long grass around them. Vicky had a peripheral awareness of Flynn's attention on her, but something else had just caught her eye. A quick glance at Flynn and she saw him just about to open his mouth. Before he could speak, she clamped her hand across the lower half of his face and pressed a finger to her pursed lips. Vicky pointed up the hill. Nestling in amongst the long grass—some of the lush green blades in its twitching mouth—sat a rabbit. With its long ears pulled back, it chewed on the grass and looked around, oblivious to the owners of two hungry bellies as they watched their potential dinner.

The action burned Vicky's knees, but she slowly lowered herself and pulled Flynn down with her. Out of the rabbit's line of sight, she spoke in a whisper. "Get the catapult out. Time for your next lesson."

So hungry it hurt, Vicky fought the urge to take the catapult from Flynn and do it herself. He needed to learn. Out in the open, anything could happen to her at any time. If she didn't teach this kid how to survive, she'd be condemning him to death.

A shake ran through Flynn's hand as he pulled the catapult from his bag. She'd seen him pick up stones since she gave him the weapon, and now she watched him load it with a perfectly round one. Even harder to let him do it now he'd produced the perfect projectile, Vicky bit her tongue and let him do what he needed to. As the boy adjusted his stance, Vicky looked down to see another smooth stone by her right foot. She lifted it up and rolled it between her fingers as she instructed the boy.

So close to him, Vicky could smell the musty reek of dirt that he carried in his hair. The bathroom container they'd set up did enough to maintain a level of hygiene, but everyone had an unpleasant scent now. "Okay, you need to pull the elastic tight before you lift the catapult."

The shake hadn't left Flynn as he pulled back the loaded weapon and lifted it out in front of him.

"Now close one eye."

Flynn did that.

"Breathe. Really calm yourself, try to slow your heart down so you can hold the catapult as steady as possible. Get the rabbit in your sights, and then …."

Before Vicky could say anything else, the *thwack* of the catapult's elastic sounded out as Flynn loosed the perfect stone.

Were it a cow, then he may have hit it. Maybe. A house he would have had no problem with. What a time to find out that the boy had a fucking terrible shot!

The rabbit took off up the road away from them. In one fluid movement, Vicky grabbed the catapult from Flynn, loaded it with the smooth stone in her hand, stood up, and let the stone fly with another *thwack*.

The white flag of the rabbit's tail bobbed up and down until Vicky scored a direct hit on the small creature's head. The satisfying *thud* of the stone connected with the animal's skull, and it rolled over and over.

Vicky ran to the thing, the steep incline draining her energy and the long grass whipping at her legs. The rabbit could recover at any second, and they couldn't go without food any longer. Like a fish out of water, the small creature twisted on the hard road. It kicked and turned, disorientated and dazed.

When Vicky lifted it up, it twisted in her grip in a palsied attempt to writhe free.

Flynn caught up a second later, so Vicky handed the creature to him.

At first, he held it at arm's length as if afraid to touch it.

"You need to get a proper grip on it otherwise it'll kick free. Grab its head tight."

Although he winced as he did it, Flynn followed Vicky's instructions and covered the rabbit's head with his grip.

"Okay," Vicky said, "now pull as hard as you can. You need to break its neck to put it out of its misery."

It looked like Flynn wanted to argue, but he didn't. Instead, he screwed his face up and pulled; although, not very hard.

"Come on, Flynn. This isn't a game anymore. If you can't kill a rabbit, you'll die."

With a clenched jaw, Flynn bared his teeth and grunted as he pulled harder this time. The rabbit's neck broke with a *pop* and Flynn dropped the creature a second later. It hit the ground hard, its dead body limp.

After Vicky had picked it up, she wrapped a piece of string around its feet and tied the other end to her belt.

Vicky only realised she'd chased the rabbit to the brow of the hill they'd been climbing once she'd stopped and taken in their surroundings. Their position afforded them a view of the town below. From where she stood, it looked like a normal town. The streets and buildings looked overgrown, but from their distance, she couldn't tell by quite how much.

As she squinted against the lowering sun, Vicky saw an old farm about a mile away. "There," she said as she pointed down at it, "that's where we'll stay tonight."

She tapped Flynn on the back, said "Come on", and jogged off in the direction of the farm.

Flynn looked far from happy about it, but he followed her down the steep hill anyway.

Chapter Nineteen

If Vicky kept Flynn moving, then he wouldn't have time to think about his family. Who was she kidding? She needed the physical distraction as much as he did. With a parasitic guilt gnawing away at her about Larissa, if she stopped to think about it for too long, it could tear her apart. But Larissa didn't matter at that moment. She looked at Flynn by her side; he didn't look back. Instead, he remained focused on the town at the bottom of the hill.

Both Flynn's terrible shot at the rabbit, and then having to kill it afterwards had clearly drained him. The boy seemed close to drowning in his depression. Just keeping him alive would be hard enough, if he fell off the precipice into despair …

Logic dictated that running downhill would be a hell of a lot easier. However, it could prove fatal if one of them slipped and fell. An injury had the potential to ruin everything. Even as they walked, each heavy footfall sent a jolt through Vicky's body. Fire burned in her knees and threw stabbing pains all the way up her back to the base of her neck. To stop, or even slow down, would take the strains off her body, but they had to keep moving.

The grass that grew up through the road not only whipped at their shins, but it left the road surface raised and uneven. Unable to track every potential lump and bump that could throw her to the ground, Vicky looked at the town below instead. Hopefully she wouldn't fall over.

So vast, the large town at the bottom of the hill spread out in either direction. Home lay on the other side, so they'd have to go through it. Like the high street, they couldn't afford to go around, and it wouldn't be any safer if they did. Regardless of which route they took, they'd be vulnerable until they were behind a reinforced and locked door.

Sweat stung Vicky's eyes, so she drew her sleeve across her forehead. As she marched, she fought to keep her breathing level and blinked against the salty itch that blurred her vision. Although they had to get through the town, it made sense to go in the morning when they had a good chance of doing the journey without it getting dark.

Now they'd gotten much closer to the farm at the bottom of the hill, Vicky saw that it had no farmhouse; it was just three barns, each seemingly dropped in a field with little regard for the position of the others around it. Surely that worked in their favour. With no house to loot, the barns had a much better chance of remaining empty because they wouldn't attract any attention from either the diseased or other survivors. Home seemed safe, but if there were other survivors out in the wild, who knew what they'd gone through—and would be prepared to do—to survive.

Still spring, the strong wind and setting sun lowered the temperature enough to pull Vicky's sweating skin taut and lift goosebumps along her arms. Without their blankets from the shipping containers, they'd have a cold night.

The sound of Flynn's heavy breaths next to Vicky forced her to look over at him.

With his mouth stretched wide as if to pull as much oxygen as he could into his body, Flynn looked back.

"You need to get in better shape," Vicky said. "All we have now are our wits and fitness, and we need to spend all of our time sharpening both of them. You understand?"

Although the boy didn't speak, he nodded. His red face glistened with sweat.

"I reckon we'll be at the barns in about ten minutes. Can you keep it up for that much longer?"

Flynn didn't reply as he continued his quick pace. But no reply had to be better than a refusal.

"Good," Vicky said, and she returned her attention to the barns halfway down the hill, and then the town beyond it. From this far away, the large built up area seemed quiet. But looks could be very fucking deceiving.

Chapter Twenty

Vicky damn near fell into the barn when they finally reached it. Exhausted from the day, her legs shook as she crossed the concrete in front of it and entered the smallest building of the three in the field. It looked the least desirable, so hopefully she'd gauged it correctly and they'd be left the fuck alone. They didn't need anyone stumbling upon them. Not that she'd seen many other people of late. In the past decade, they'd only seen one other party once. They'd been far away and walking through a field. Vicky and Rhys hid away from them until they passed. Over the years, Vicky had run through that scenario and played it out differently in her mind.

Only a few months after they'd moved into the containers, how could she have known she'd be there for another ten years and they wouldn't see anyone else? Had she known at the time, she would have invited the hikers to join them. Maybe then none of the fucked up shit would have happened. They had the space too; they could have started their *own* community. She gulped against the rising feeling of guilt; hopefully the walkers arrived safely wherever they were heading to.

Vicky and Flynn's footsteps against the barn's dusty floor called out through what seemed to be an empty space. When Vicky pushed the door closed behind them, it groaned, the hinges rusty from years of inaction. At about halfway closed, the hinges seized. Although she may have been able to close it some more, it would make too much noise.

When Flynn grabbed one of his bag's shoulder straps as if to remove it, Vicky wagged a finger at him. Now trapped in a barn, she spoke in a near whisper. "Don't put your stuff down yet. You need to be able to move in a flash. Retrieving your bag could be the difference between life and death."

Slack with exhaustion, Flynn's shoulders sagged as he stared at Vicky and continued to fight for breath. Despite no reply, he kept his rucksack on.

"We need to start a fire," Vicky said. "Gather up dry kindling." She looked around them. "It looks like there are enough twigs and dry grass to get something going."

***

It only took a few minutes for them to form a small pile. The grass, balled like tumbleweed, had been a find. Without it, the process would have been a lot harder.

Early on in her scavenging with Rhys, Vicky had found a flint in a camping store. When she kneeled down near the fire, Flynn crouched down next to her. She untied the rabbit from her belt and laid it on the floor next to the pile of kindling.

With evening settling in, the barn had grown darker, so when Vicky sparked the flint, the magnesium blink left a stain on her vision. Each strike of the flint dazzled her more than the last, but she continued to send small sparks into the dry pile on the floor.

When a large spark landed in the middle of the grass, Vicky patted Flynn's shoulder. "Right, blow on it."

Although Flynn cooked when they were back at the containers, he rarely started the fires, but he knew what to do. He leaned down and blew gently. The spark glowed bright. He drew a breath and blew again. This time, the spark glowed even brighter.

As she watched the boy, careful as he nurtured the fire, Vicky placed a gentle hand on his back. She didn't have any words of wisdom for him. How could she comfort him about the loss of both of his parents? But she could encourage him. "That's it, Flynn. Keep blowing."

As Flynn coaxed the fire to life, Vicky stood up and stretched some of the aches from her back and knees. She pushed her pelvis forward as a line of pops ran up her spine, and breathed in the woody smell of the fire.

Smoke curled up from the ground, and each of Flynn's blows made the grass glow brighter. A look around showed it seemed to be clear, and although inside a barn, Vicky could never be sure. Even though the place offered some protection, it restricted Vicky's view of anything that may want to attack them. But then again, who wanted to sleep out in the open? Especially as the cold evening set in. They had to rely on faith to keep them safe for that night. No matter how hard Vicky tried, she couldn't minimise all of the risks in life.

After she'd picked the rabbit up from the floor, Vicky watched the first flames catch on the fire and Flynn move back from it. When he stood up, he smiled at her.

The smile fell when Vicky handed him the rabbit. Another kitchen duty that had never been given to him, Flynn said, "You want *me* to skin it?"

"You need to be able to do everything now, Flynn."

She could have been pushing him too hard. Maybe he didn't need to do everything right now, but he needed something to keep him busy. An inactive body could lead to an overactive mind. When they arrived at Home he could fall apart, but not now. Unless Home turned out to be something completely different to what it promised—not that they had any other options beyond that anyway.

Flynn held the limp rabbit and stared at it.

"Tear the skin by its knees and push the knees through," Vicky said.

The same face he'd pulled when he broke the rabbit's neck twisted his features.

"Come on, Flynn, you *need* to be able to do this."

His hand shook again as he dug his fingers into one of the rabbit's knees. With a clenched jaw, he pulled a tear in the rabbit's skin. He then bent the creature's leg and pushed its knee through. Although he may not have been comfortable doing it, he had seen it done a thousand times before and it showed.

Once he'd slipped both of the knees out, Flynn tore the skin so it detached from the feet. He wrapped a tight grip around the animal's ankles and pulled the skin down.

Vicky watched Flynn's horrified expression and shook her head at him. "Come on, Flynn, it's only a rabbit. Man the fuck up, yeah?"

Flynn didn't reply as he continued to pull the skin off.

With half of the skin removed, Flynn paused to look up at Vicky. His eyes glistened from his clear distress.

"You've lived a sheltered life, boy."

Flynn didn't reply.

***

Although she'd eaten a lot of rabbit over the past decade, Vicky's mouth watered as she chewed on the gamey meat. Each gulp sated the hollowness in her stomach. Since they'd taken the rabbit off the spit, the pair hadn't spoken to one another. When Vicky looked up at Flynn, she waited for him to look back and smiled. "I'm glad you finally managed to skin the rabbit. I thought I'd starve to death watching you earlier."

"Fuck you!" Flynn said.

The outburst forced Vicky to pull her head back. "I *beg* your pardon?"

Flynn's mouth buckled and he started to cry. "I said, fuck you! Fuck you and what you're saying to me. I've lost my mum and dad, the last thing I need is you giving me a bollocking too. I'm trying my hardest, Vicky; you need to go easier on me."

It tore at Vicky's heart to see him that way, but she said it anyway. "Actually, me being harsh is *exactly* what you need. I understand that you're hurting; I'm hurting too, but we *need* to survive." Vicky's eyes itched with the burn of tears. "We can't afford to grieve right now. I'm sorry, Flynn, I truly am, but we need to keep going. We need to find somewhere safe before we deal with anything else. To find somewhere safe, we need to survive. And if you can't skin a fucking rabbit—"

Flynn, red-faced and with a fierce scowl, drew a deep breath as if to launch into a tirade. But before he could speak, the sound of clumsy footsteps approached the barn's entrance.

As one, Vicky and Flynn turned to see three diseased burst through the barn's door. All three of them—twisted with the virus—fixed on the pair with their dark stares.

Chapter Twenty-One

A wet slap pulled Vicky's attention away from the diseased for the briefest second. Flynn's part-eaten bit of rabbit lay on the dusty floor next to the fire, and he stood, slack-jawed, as he stared at the monsters in the doorway.

A quick scan of the barn and Vicky spotted the mezzanine hayloft. Instead of a rickety old ladder, a set of stairs led up to the next level. The higher ground would give them some advantage. "Go up there," Vicky said to Flynn. She then saw the skylight in the ceiling. "Get out on the roof."

The boy didn't need to be told twice. With his bag still on his back, he took off and sprinted toward the staircase that would take him away from the diseased, if only temporarily.

But Vicky didn't follow him.

Although the smallest of the barns, it could still easily hold two football fields. In the centre of it with the stairs at her back, Vicky stood between the diseased and Flynn.

Flynn's movement seemed to spark the three diseased to life, and they rushed forward as one.

The *snap* of Vicky's baton called out in the barn, and she

dropped into her usual defensive crouch as she waited for them. Not that she planned on dying that day, but if she could give Flynn the best chance, she would. Whatever happened, he *would* survive. She owed that to his parents.

Vicky glanced behind and saw Flynn had reached the stairs. His footsteps echoed a rapid beat in the cavernous space as he made his way up. When Vicky spun back toward the door, she did it just in time to bring her baton around on the diseased at the front of the three. It sent the creature sprawling, and she jumped aside to avoid the other two.

The one she'd knocked down twisted and writhed as it dealt with the heavy blow to its head as Vicky readied herself for its mates.

Clumsy in their movement, they both pulled up and turned around to face her. They screamed louder than they had before. Their rage echoed through the barn, and they sprinted back toward Vicky.

Although she had her baton raised ready to fight, Vicky caught sight of the others at the barn's door. More than three this time, they'd obviously heard the call. With a dry throat and sweating palms, Vicky waited until the last moment before she darted out of the way of the two diseased for a second time.

Although Vicky moved like a matador, her luck wouldn't last. When a stream of diseased funnelled into the warehouse, she left the other two behind, jumped over the one that remained on the floor, and made a bee-line for the stairs Flynn had run up.

As she fought for breath, she looked up to see Flynn at the top. Clearly concerned for her wellbeing, he'd stopped and looked down at her.

"Run," Vicky cried. "Get that window smashed."

With the onset of evening, the window glowed a deep red from the low sun. Much later in the day, and they wouldn't have been able to see anything in the barn.

When she reached the stairs, Vicky ran up them two at a time. About twice the height of a normal flight of stairs in a house, she pushed on up, her thighs on fire, her bag heavy on her back.

Once at the top on the mezzanine, she looked down at the diseased on their tail. The new batch of them streamed into the warehouse in a seemingly never-ending line. With every new body that entered the building, their collective scream grew louder. The chaos made Vicky's head spin, and she had to rest against the wall for stability.

When the first of the diseased hit the bottom of the stairs, Vicky took off after Flynn.

At no more than a metre wide, the walkway that led around the side of the barn had no railing for safety. Too many of the diseased on it at one time would be sure to see some of them fall over the side to the hard ground below.

As she ran along the walkway, Vicky saw Flynn reach the window in the roof at the other end.

The sound of the diseased may have chased her, but Vicky kept her focus on Flynn as he grabbed his baseball bat with both hands and forced the end of it into the glass window.

The pane broke with a *crash* and Flynn jumped back as it rained glass down on him.

When he looked to Vicky, she made a shooing motion with her hand. "Get out on the roof, now!"

A look behind showed Vicky the diseased had reached the mezzanine level. The ones in the front raced after her along the walkway. When she glanced at Flynn again, she saw his foot disappear as he climbed out of the window. It best fucking work, because if it didn't, she had no more ideas.

The walkway shook beneath Vicky's feet from the stampede of the diseased. It trembled like it would fall to the ground. Hopefully, it would hold for as long as she needed it.

Just metres from the window, Vicky kept her attention in front of her. To look behind would slow her down and she couldn't afford to slow down. With her limbs working like pistons, she listened as the occasional scream and thud signalled yet another diseased had fallen from the walkway.

The end of Flynn's baseball bat suddenly poked in through the window from outside. "What the fuck?" Vicky called. Then she got it. The boy ran the end of his bat around the inside of the window frame to remove the shards of glass that he'd no doubt contended with. An urgent escape could lead to a shredded Vicky, and that wouldn't help anyone.

Just as Vicky got to the window, Flynn pulled his bat away and she jumped out onto the sloped, corrugated roof.

Made from thin metal, but not so thin that it wouldn't hold them, the roof ran away from the window in both directions. Vicky clambered up toward the apex.

A second later, the first of the diseased jumped out after her. Steep in its gradient, the roof seemed too steep for the first uncoordinated fuck bag. After two steps, it slipped and rolled down the side.

As she fought to get her breath back, Vicky watched the

flailing body gather momentum before it reached the end of the roof and disappeared. Its scream ended with a thud against the concrete ground below.

***

Cold from where the sun had set, the sky dark around them, Vicky shifted on the roof's apex to try to find some comfort. She'd tried straddling it for a time, but it made her hips ache. Whichever way she positioned herself, it didn't help; the roof hadn't been designed to be sat on. When she stood up and looked over the edge, her head spun. She rode it out for a few seconds as she watched the diseased continue to rush into the barn.

A hundred or so fell from the roof and did everything they could to get back in to try again. Some survived the fall. Others didn't—or at least, it broke them to a point where they couldn't attempt another run.

It would have been comical had it not dragged on for so fucking long.

With the sting of fatigue in her eyes, Vicky blinked against her heavy eyelids and watched a diseased she'd seen at least three other times. It crawled through the window; its body a mangled mess of fractures and breaks. It looked up at her and Flynn, screamed, reached out, and slipped again as it tumbled off the roof.

"Surely we won't see that one again," Flynn said.

"I thought that *last* time," Vicky replied.

Of the scores that tried, several of the diseased had made it a little way up the roof toward the pair. They'd received a baton to the face for their troubles and soon followed the others down and off the side.

"Keep an eye out," Vicky said as she lay back against the roof and pushed her hips to the sky to try to relieve the pains in her body. As she rocked back and fourth, she looked out over the dark countryside. With the only light coming from the moon, Vicky sighed. "I hope Home's what it says it is."

"Me too," Flynn said. "I can't handle living a life on the run like this."

Chapter Twenty-Two

"Shame we've got to leave really, isn't it?" Vicky said as she stared out over the fields, the breeze tossing her hair.

When Vicky felt Flynn turn to her, she faced him. Bleary-eyed from a night without sleep, he blinked repeatedly but said nothing.

Vicky looked back out over the countryside and large town below them. "Well, it is. Look at this view. When you take a moment to see what's happened to this part of the world in the past decade, it reminds you how powerful nature is …"

"… and just how beautiful," Flynn finished for her.

A patchwork of fields—all with overgrown bushes and long grass—swayed in the early morning breeze. Roads were tinted green from where nature had reclaimed them. Before long, they wouldn't even be roads anymore. When Vicky looked at the large town in front of them again, anxiety tightened in her stomach. The most sensible option would be to go straight through the middle. They'd get through so much quicker. The least amount of time they spent out in the open, the better. They needed to get to Home. That's what she'd told Flynn, and it made sense, but regardless of the logic, the tense rock in her stomach balled tighter and lurched at the sight of the sheer volume of abandoned buildings. It gave the diseased a lot of places to hide.

When Vicky looked down at the ground, she saw just a few diseased below still flailing among the mass of limp bodies. The lemming conveyor belt that had climbed out of the window and plummeted to their death had finally stopped a few hours ago, but the pair had to wait until now to move. With morning lighting up the world, they could finally see the damage below and formulate an escape plan.

Although a couple of diseased squirmed on the ground, they didn't look like they could walk. The fall must have shattered their legs or spines in some way. As they dragged themselves around, Vicky nudged Flynn. "You've got some stones for your catapult, right?"

The boy said nothing, so when Vicky turned to look at him, she saw he'd turned pale as he bit down on his bottom lip. "I didn't think," he said.

"You need to *start* thinking, Flynn. Why the fuck would you walk around with a catapult and no stones?"

The boy shook his head. "I'm sorry, Vicky, I just didn't think."

"Not an excuse."

Silence hung between them until Vicky pulled some smooth stones from her pocket and handed them to him. Whenever she saw a stone that would work well in the catapult, she'd pick it up, so she always had a supply. "Here, take these. Now it's time for target practice. I can see two diseased down there; I want you to take them out with a headshot each."

After Flynn had shifted down the roof to get closer to the edge, he took one of the smooth stones and loaded up the catapult.

"You're pulling the elastic at an angle," Vicky said. "You need to be straighter."

Although aware of the harshness of her tone, she didn't care. This boy may need to survive on his own at some point. He needed to learn, and he needed to do it fast.

Flynn tried to straighten the elastic, but it looked no better. The kid would struggle to hit the barn next to them if he held the catapult like that. But Vicky said nothing as she watched him pull the stone back a little more, and then let fly with a *thwip.* The stone kicked up dust about five metres away from one of the diseased's head, and Vicky sighed.

He tried again with another stone and missed the second one by a similar distance.

After she'd tutted at him, Vicky leaned forward, took the catapult from him, and loaded it with a stone she had in her supply.

"Look," she said as she closed one eye and pulled the elastic back. "You need to make sure you pull it back straight, so when you let it go, the stone flies true."

The elastic made a *thwack* noise as she loosed the stone and she hit one of the diseased directly in the temple. She reloaded the catapult and passed it back to Flynn.

With a deep frown of concentration, Flynn tried to copy Vicky. He missed again.

Vicky took the catapult back from him. "That was better."

Another shot, and she hit the second diseased before she handed the catapult back to Flynn.

***

The morning dew that coated the barn's metal roof made it more hazardous to slide down than it had been to climb. While remaining on her bottom, Vicky shifted down a foot at a time, the dew soaking through her trousers and knickers. It may not have been comfortable to be so damp, but the wet fabric gave her more grip as she shimmied down the roof.

When they got to the broken window, Vicky turned to Flynn. "I'll go in first, and you follow behind. We don't know how many of the fuckers are left. I'm hoping that if there are any they won't move much, and we can easily beat them. You need to be ready to follow me in and fight, okay?"

Flynn nodded, but it gave Vicky zero confidence. Maybe he simply didn't have a fighting instinct in him, but she had to give him the chance to prove he could do it.

Vicky slipped through the window and landed on the walkway with a *thud*. The shock of the landing snapped through her tired body. A few groans came from within the dark barn. With her baton raised, she waited, poised and ready to go. But nothing came at her.

A second later, Flynn dropped down next to her. He landed louder than she had and with far less grace. With her heart in her throat, Vicky waited for her pulse to settle before leading him across the walkway.

As they moved through the dark space, Vicky's eyes adjusted to the dim light. The walkway seemed free of the diseased, but some lay down below from where they'd clearly fallen. As broken as the ones outside, they lay on the floor, no more active than large slugs. They posed no threat, so Vicky wouldn't waste the energy killing them.

***

When they stepped out of the barn's front door, Vicky looked at the two diseased she'd hit with the catapult. None of the others moved. Maybe the getaway would be easier than—

The thudding of clumsy footsteps sounded behind her. She spun around to see a large diseased man no more than two metres away. Too slow to lift her baton, she pulled away from her attacker and raised her hands in front of her face. With her eyes closed, she waited for the burn of his teeth to bite into her flesh.

Chapter Twenty-Three

A loud *tock* and Vicky watched the huge diseased fall to one side and hit the ground cheek first. Flynn followed up his first swing as he brought his bat down on the fat fuck's head.

A fresh waft of shit lifted up from the corpse as if it had defecated where it lay, and Vicky screwed her nose up as she backed away from it. Adrenaline surged through her as she looked at Flynn. The boy stood as if he expected praise. But he wouldn't get it; he had a long fucking way to go and a lot to learn before she would praise him. Although, as she looked at his expectant face …

"Thanks," she said. Before he could reply, she added, "Come on, let's get out of here."

***

Everything ached. With no sleep and a heavy backpack on, Vicky sweated in the strong sun and winced with every step.

When she saw a bench, nearly hidden by the long grass that surrounded it, she moved over to it and sat down. Flynn came and sat down next to her. When he went to take his bag off his back, Vicky raised a halting hand at him. How many times would she have to tell him?

Flynn frowned at her, but nodded and kept the pack on.

"Remember what I said about taking your backpack off? You need to be able to move at a moment's notice. If you'd have put it down like you'd wanted to in the barn, then you may not have it now."

Although the boy sighed, he didn't reply. Vicky shook her head to herself.

As they sat on the bench halfway down the huge hill, the morning sun beat down on them, and Vicky looked out over the large town. They'd be there in an hour or two, and they'd have to make a decision then. Despite what she'd said to Flynn, Vicky hadn't convinced herself yet. Did they go through the town or around it?

Birds rode the currents above Vicky's and Flynn's heads. To watch them meant looking into the sun, but Vicky did it anyway and her vision blurred with her tears.

Maybe Rhys and Larissa looked over them at that moment. When Vicky looked across at Flynn, she saw he looked up too. His eyes also watered. With his face fixed up at the sky, he bit his quivering bottom lip.

To look at Flynn made Vicky's throat ache. She shifted over and put an arm around his broad shoulders. He smelled of sweat and dirt. No doubt Vicky had the same tang to her. "I would have stayed, you know."

The boy looked at her but said nothing as he cried.

"After your dad died, that changed everything."

More tears ran down Flynn's face, and his lip buckled out of shape.

"I wouldn't have left and expected you and your mum to cope on your own. Your mum didn't need to go out scavenging."

After he'd nodded several times, Flynn gulped. "I know you would have stayed." It took a couple more seconds for him to get his other words out. "Mum didn't know that though."

Vicky sighed. Flynn had every right to be angry with her. She hadn't communicated her intentions to Larissa, and if she had, things may be very different now. With her arm still around him, she swallowed the guilt that sat as a lump in her throat, pulled Flynn in closer to her, and kissed the top of his dirty head. "We'll be okay. We'll get through this."

He sighed, but he didn't pull away. Nor did he reply.

***

An amount of time passed, fuck knows how long, but long enough for Vicky to seize up like a rusty hinge. Deep aches sat in every muscle and joint, and tiredness pulled on her facial muscles.

"The worst is yet to come," she said.

Flynn pulled out of her hug and looked at her. "Huh?"

After she'd nodded at the large town, she said, "Going through there." When her stomach rumbled, she instinctively grabbed it. "I'm still hungry too. The rabbit I ate will keep me going, but I need more food."

"Why don't we go around the town? There's no rush to get to Home. We can take our time, can't we?" Flynn then added, "If we're careful, I mean."

The warmth of the sun soaked into Vicky's face as she watched the town below. "I don't know about you, but I think the less time we spend out in the open, the better. If we go through the town, we cut our travel time by two-thirds, maybe more."

Before Flynn could respond, Vicky pulled the wind-up radio from her pocket. The click of the mechanism popped as Vicky spun the wheel on the back of the device. When she'd fully wound it, she checked the volume had been set to low, and lifted it up so both she and Flynn could listen to it.

"Home is a place where we're beginning to fight back. Hiding isn't working. We need to build an army. We need to take the battle to the diseased. We have plenty of people already. We have running water and warm showers. We have electricity and food to go around. We have plenty of food. Able bodied or not; we will *take you in. Home is located just near Britnall. The diseased can't read, so we have signs to guide the way. Everyone is welcome. Please come and join us. You don't have to go hungry or thirsty any longer."*

By the time Vicky had pulled the radio away from her ear, her mouth watered and her stomach rumbled. "It's a slightly different broadcast," she said. "And they have food—food and water. What if we take the long way 'round, and we don't find either? I don't know how long I can keep going on scraps."

Silence hung between the pair as they both looked out over the large town below. The long grass swayed in the wind around them, but the town remained still and resolute. An unknown quantity, it would only reveal its cards if they committed to entering it.

"Fuck knows what's in there," Vicky said. "The only thing I'm certain of is that our route through the town will be much quicker."

Vicky glanced at Flynn and saw him staring at the town. "Come on, mate," she said, "I need your feedback. What do we do?"

For the first time since they'd sat down, Flynn straightened his back and drew a deep breath. An assertive nod as he wiped his eyes, and he said, "We go through. We can both run, right?"

After she'd patted his broad back, Vicky smiled. "Yes, we can. We can run like the fucking wind if we need to."

When Flynn removed his bag from his back, Vicky grabbed his hand. "What are you doing?"

Forceful, but gentle at the same time, Flynn removed Vicky's hand. He placed his bag on his lap so he could undo the zip. He then pulled several items from it. A woman's hat, his dad's boots, a jewellery box with a decade's worth of acquired jewellery, and Rhys's aviator sunglasses.

"W … what are you doing?" Vicky asked.

"This stuff is weighing me down." As he re-shouldered his bag, Flynn beat his fist against his chest. "I have all I need of my parents in my heart. I don't need to carry their belongings too. Or, at least, not all of their belongings. I've kept a few light bits."

Before Vicky could respond, the boy got to his feet. "Come on," he said, "let's go."

Despite the aches in her limbs, Vicky stood up too. A glance around and the area seemed clear; exposed on the side of the hill, it made it hard for anything to approach them unnoticed.

Flynn set off in the direction of the ghost town. Still and silent, it stared up the hill in defiance of their bravery. With one last look at Flynn's personal items on the bench, Vicky set off after him.

Chapter Twenty-Four

Exhausted from her lack of sleep, Vicky pushed her clumsy body on as the call of the diseased chased them. They'd not walked far down the hill before another pack of the hideous fuckers came at them. As she ran, her backpack slapped against the space between her shoulder blades. It may have only been light, but the repeated contact happened enough times to cause a stinging discomfort that would only get worse when she finally took it off. With at least ten minutes until they got to the town, they wouldn't make it before the diseased caught up with them.

There were about fifteen of them, and although some were faster than the others, they all ran with abandon. Where Vicky and Flynn had to worry about a fall down the steep hill, the diseased didn't seem to give a fuck. It worked in their favour in fact—gravity added rocket fuel to their clumsy sprint.

The uneven road had been kind to Vicky and Flynn so far. Although she couldn't take it for granted; each time her foot turned one way or the other, her heart missed a beat. The next lump or loose piece of asphalt could be the one to throw her to the ground.

A large derelict house sat in a field to their right. It looked like something ripped from a horror film. Vicky had tried to ignore it, but with just two other choices—none and fuck all—the decision had been made for them. They could lose them like they did at the barn.

They could get on the roof and defend themselves.

Slightly ahead of Flynn, Vicky suddenly changed course and shouted over her shoulder, "Follow me."

Flynn gasped as he called after her. "Where are you going?"

Vicky couldn't have a conversation now. She could barely breathe. The boy would work it out.

"Vicky," he called again.

Vicky checked behind. When she saw he'd followed her, she didn't respond.

The sun still burned bright in the sky. The heat of it, combined with the run, turned Vicky's body slick with sweat. Her collar itched, her trousers chaffed, her underwear rode up—none of that mattered with the mob behind them.

Another glance at the town at the bottom of the hill and Vicky pushed on. It pained her to deviate from their plan, but they had to survive first. They'd only make it to Home if they made sensible choices.

At less than five hundred metres from the house, Vicky looked behind again. Pain twisted through Flynn's face, but he kept his pace up enough to maintain some distance between him and the crowd behind. A woman headed the pack of diseased. With her mouth stretched wide and her cheek ripped open, Vicky could see her entire rotting jaw. Eyes that shouldn't have been able to see focused on her with what seemed to be laser-like precision. They wouldn't stop until they'd either caught them, or they'd been killed themselves.

An old detached house, the black building had been predominantly made from wood. It had clearly stood empty for the past decade at least, but quite possibly longer. Even from a few hundred metres away, Vicky could see the dirt and dust that clouded up the large windows. An old Bentley sat in the driveway. Covered in vines, the house had been claimed by nature and—like most things now—before long would be just another mound in the overgrown landscape.

When Vicky got closer to it, she saw a perimeter fence. At no more than a metre high, the grass had hidden it from view until that moment. As she vaulted it, one hand on the wooden barrier, she called behind to Flynn, "Fence."

With the house still in her sights, she heard the grunt and then heavy landing of the boy behind her. Another quick check and she saw he'd made it without any problem.

A *crash* then sounded out, followed by the deep *oof* of air leaving someone's body. Vicky turned around to see the lead diseased fall from her collision with the gate. Unfortunately, the others learned from her mistake, and they hurdled the fence.

With the grass much longer now, Vicky used her hands to push it aside so she could make a path to the house.

Tall and imposing, the house seemed like the kind of building that watched you when you entered it. Now she'd gotten closer, Vicky could see it had been converted from a barn. Wood everywhere, it had huge windows to let the outside world look in.

On any other day, Vicky would have checked the door, but

they didn't have time. Instead, she turned sideways and shoulder barged it.

Fire ripped through her body when she connected with the barrier, and the heavy jolt threw stars across her vision. But the door gave with a splintering *crack,* and she fell into the house to hit the dusty wooden floor.

Despite her pain, she got to her feet and held the door open for Flynn, who charged in a second later.

After she'd slammed the door shut, she grabbed a nearby bookcase and toppled it over to block the way in.

Flynn came over with an armchair. Gasping as he moved the heavy item, he managed to wedge it up behind the bookcase.

In what felt like seconds, they'd moved a coffee table, two dining room chairs, and a sofa up against the door. Vicky paused with her hands on her hips. At that moment, one of the diseased crashed against the outside of the door with a loud *bang.*

The only chance of survival would be on a higher floor, so Vicky pointed across the room and shouted to Flynn, "Upstairs, now."

He took off at a sprint. A deep *creak* then shuddered through the soles of Vicky's shoes. Before she could call out to him, the floor gave way with a tearing crack like a ship wrecking against jagged rocks.

The dust stung Vicky's eyes, and although she had to blink to see through it, she made out the downed form of Flynn in what must have been the house's basement. A second later, the *crash* of the large window at the front of the house exploded into the room with a tinkling of glass. The stench of the diseased rushed in with it, and Vicky stood frozen to the spot as she watched the pack come straight at her.

Chapter Twenty-Five

The dust in the air obscured Vicky's view and turned her throat dry. As she peered down at Flynn, she couldn't see where she could land, but she had a plan. When the diseased at the front of the pack reached out for her, its face shredded and bloody from where it had run through the huge glass window, Vicky jumped.

The shock of the landing ripped through Vicky and stung her knees. Despite the pain, she pushed on and rushed to Flynn.

The slap of a diseased hit the hard floor behind her as it followed her down without hesitation.

This basement had clearly never been used for anything other than storage. Although, with the thick reek of damp—so strong it masked the stench of the diseased—it probably couldn't have been used even for that.

"Get up," Vicky shouted at Flynn and pointed toward the small corridor that must have led to the stairs up and out of the basement.

Flynn didn't need to be told twice. In one fluid movement, he jumped to his feet and sprinted in the direction she'd pointed to.

The *crack* of body after body hit the ground in the basement behind them as the diseased that had chased them poured over the edge into the dingy space.

Flynn disappeared from sight for a few seconds before Vicky followed him around the corner. She'd called it correctly from what she'd seen up above. They had a chance.

Flynn reached the top of the stairs by the time Vicky arrived at the bottom. When he grabbed the door to get out of there, it didn't move. He turned and looked down at her. "It's locked."

As she snapped her baton out to its full length, Vicky turned her back on Flynn and ascended the stairs backwards. "I thought it would be."

"Then why did you tell me to come this way?"

Before she could answer, the first of the diseased appeared around the corner. Not only shredded from the window, it limped as if hurt from the drop into the basement. Yet it still moved toward Vicky and snapped its jaws.

"What the fuck are we going to do?" Flynn called out.

But Vicky didn't respond. Sure, her heart beat so fast it damn near exploded, but she had a plan and it would work.

When the first diseased had climbed up a few stairs—the others backed up behind it in a line because of the narrow corridor that led up the stairs—Vicky swung for it with her baton and scored a direct hit on the top of its head.

The creature fell to her blow, and the next diseased climbed over it.

With a clinched jaw, Vicky drove the baton as an uppercut into the monster's chin. She knocked it back and it fell over the top of the first into the others behind.

The next diseased appeared and Vicky yelled out as she dealt yet another fierce blow.

***

The diseased moved forward as a rising tide. Slow, but unrelenting, they came toward Vicky. She hit every one of them with her baton. Sweat ran into her eyes and her arms had turned to lead, but she pushed through her discomfort and persevered.

Another heavy whack sent another one of the diseased stumbling backwards.

Silence followed. Vicky fought to catch her breath and watched the pile of fallen bodies at the bottom of the stairs.

When none of them moved, she finally turned back to Flynn. "The three hundred Spartans."

Even in the dark, Vicky saw Flynn's frown. "There's a Greek myth," she said, "about how three hundred Spartans fought off a vast Persian army. It's said they led the Persians into a narrow pass, where they slaughtered them. Because it funnelled their enemy into a tight space, it rendered their numbers useless. The Spartans, who already had superior fighting skills, only needed stamina to win the battle at that point."

Another deep breath and Vicky broke into a coughing fit. The dust in the air ran straight to the back of her throat, and she heaved with every wet bark that flipped through her. When she recovered, she stood up straight and smiled. "Not that I have the stamina of a Spartan warrior, but it looks like I had enough to beat about fifteen diseased."

Still clearly shaken from the ordeal, Flynn watched Vicky with wide eyes. A warble rattled his voice. "Thank you. I thought I was done for when I fell."

Giving him a sharp nod, Vicky stepped past Flynn. With a two-step run up, she shoulder-barged the basement door open and fell out into the old barn conversion. Her baton raised, she did a quick scan of the place. It seemed empty.

Vicky led the way around the side of the hole in the floor.

"More than fifteen. I'd say double that," Flynn said as he looked down at the diseased in the basement.

Vicky laughed. "Good job I didn't realise that at the time." She winked. "I would have left you for dead had I known."

Chapter Twenty-Six

"Hey," Flynn said as he ran over to an old wooden pole, "look at this."

Vicky followed him over. "Oh … My … God. I could kiss you, Flynn."

"It's okay, you don't need to."

Vicky laughed at his red cheeks as she removed the bottle from the bottom of the funnel. "Your dad and I used to do this to collect water too. The bottle's full, so whoever set this up must have moved on." A shake ran through Vicky's hands as she pulled the bottle free and handed it to Flynn. She watched Flynn drink, her mouth drier than ever with the prospect of fluid in front of her.

After Flynn pulled the bottle away and gasped, he handed it to Vicky, who held it up to the light. He'd had at least half of it. Just before she drank it, she looked at Flynn again. "To Rhys and Larissa."

Although Flynn nodded, he didn't reply. Instead, he pulled his shoulders back and clamped his jaw tight.

Vicky then drained the rest of the bottle. Despite its muddy taste, the water stretched to every dry part of her mouth and she released a satisfied groan.

In the moments that followed their drink, both Vicky and Flynn stood in silence and looked out over the town they were heading toward. Although nothing like London in size, it looked large enough; especially when they had to travel through it by foot.

"I think going through it is the sensible option," Vicky said as she stored the empty bottle in her backpack. "If we can move fast, we can rest when we get to the other side. We'll be much closer to Home by then too."

Flynn stared into the city with pursed lips and a pale face.

Vicky rocked from side to side. It did little to ease the aches in her hips, back, knees … hell, every fucking part of her ached.

Although she knew he hated it, Vicky reached over and ruffled Flynn's hair. "Come on, champ, let's do this."

The teenage boy blew his greasy hair from his eyes and raised an eyebrow in Vicky's direction.

Despite her exhaustion, Vicky laughed for the second time in as many minutes. "Thank you," she said.

"For what?"

She laughed some more. "Just thanks. Come on, let's go."

***

Like everything else in this world, nature had claimed the sign that read *WELCOME TO FOXSTEAD*.

A shake of her head and Vicky turned to Flynn as they walked into the town. "This place used to be rammed full of arseholes. Right on the commuter belt, the city wankers earned all their money in London and came to live out here. When London got too dangerous to spend any leisure time in—terrorist attacks, muggings, armed robberies—everyone who could afford it moved out to towns like this. They went into London for business and left for pleasure. London became a rat hole on the weekends that very few people visited for fun. All large houses with high gates, the four-by-four crowd loved it here."

"Four-by-four?"

"Oh, sorry. I forget you've spent most of your life in a shipping container. There was an all-terrain vehicle, that would probably be pretty fucking useful now, and it was called a four-by-four. Anyway, a lot of the rich mums had them to take their offspring to school in. Back in the day,"—Vicky kicked a particularly stubborn tuft of grass that had sprung up from the middle of the road—"these roads were so smooth you could roll a marble down them."

"So they didn't need the four-by-fours." Flynn said.

Vicky laughed. "Exactly! Nice cars, but they ended up becoming a symbol of pretension rather than anything else."

As if to highlight her point, Vicky looked to her right at the first large house in the town and a huge rusted out Land Rover sat in the driveway. "That's one there."

"It doesn't look very practical."

Four flat tyres, mould around the window seals, and rust spots all over the bodywork, Vicky laughed again. "It would have ten years ago."

By the time they'd passed the next house on the opposite side of the road, the mood had darkened and a chill snapped through

Vicky. Everything seemed to get quieter inside the town.

A glance across at Flynn and Vicky saw him look around. "I've got a bad feeling, Vicky."

"Have you had a good feeling since you've left the containers?"

"Well, no, but it feels much worse now. How do we even know that Home is legitimate? What if it's a trap?"

"It could be, but why would they want to trap us?"

"Maybe they want to eat us?"

Because they were surrounded by harder surfaces than before, when Vicky laughed, it echoed down the abandoned street. It took any mirth from her response as she watched for signs of movement potentially disturbed by her sound. "This ain't the movies, Flynn."

When she saw his vacant look, Vicky elaborated. "People don't eat people when they can plant veg and shit. Why the fuck would they?"

Flynn didn't reply, and near silence hung between the pair. Other than the scrape of their shoes over the craggy road, Vicky heard nothing. It made it harder to ignore the feeling of being watched. She snapped her head around to look at another house beside them. Grass grew up the walls, the gate lay broken from where it had fallen from its hinges, and the dark windows stared back at her. Anything could be in there. Without a word to Flynn, she picked up her pace and Flynn seemed more than happy to follow.

Chapter Twenty-Seven

The pair said very little to one another as they walked through the deserted town. They navigated a rat run of streets with abandoned houses on either side of them—or houses that *appeared* to be abandoned.

When Vicky spoke, she saw Flynn jump. "One good thing about the diseased is that they let us know they're coming. The clumsy fuckers couldn't sneak up on shit."

"I still feel like we're being watched."

"You're not helping, Flynn." It would have been easy for Vicky to discount what he'd said if she didn't feel the same.

Flynn shrugged.

When she saw an entrance to the back of a large school, Vicky pointed at it. "Let's go through there."

"Why?"

"There has to be some open spaces in there. At least if we're walking alongside a school field, nothing will be able to take us by surprise."

The boy looked like he wanted to argue with her. When he didn't, Vicky took the lead and guided them through the entrance to what the sign told them was *The Coach Park*.

As they walked up the long driveway, Vicky looked at the school. A hockey pitch on their right, she hadn't given it a second thought until Flynn gasped. The sharp outburst sent her pulse skyrocketing, and she dropped into a defensive crouch.

As Flynn stared at the hockey pitch, his jaw loose, he said, "We need to get out of here."

"Why?"

He pointed at the pitch. "Someone's been here recently, look how short the grass is."

"I'm glad I brought you along; for comedy value, if nothing else."

Genuine confusion crushed Flynn's face.

"That's Astroturf."

"What's Astroturf?"

He had a point. Why would he have seen it before now? And even if he had seen it, he would have been too little to know what it was. "Fake grass, Flynn. It's used on all-weather sports pitches like this one so people can play sport on it all year 'round."

With the same confused frown on his face, Flynn dropped his head with a sigh. "Sorry."

"For what?"

"For being such an idiot."

Vicky had been too harsh on him. "You're not an idiot; you have a lot of questions because you've been living away from everything for most of your life. I'm sorry, I should be more understanding."

***

When they reached the large open area of asphalt that must have been used for coaches a long time ago, Vicky looked around. A huge sports hall stood on the other side, and it led down into what looked like the main part of the school. It had to be more cramped down that way. If they went the other way, it looked like they'd pass the sports fields.

Before Vicky could ask Flynn which way he thought they should go, she stopped and grabbed his arm.

Flynn stopped next to her.

"Pass me the catapult."

As he fished the weapon from his pocket, Flynn looked around. When he saw what Vicky had seen, he stopped. "Shall I try?"

"We don't have time for you to try at the moment, Flynn. We can practice your skills when we're out of this shit-hole town. And when I'm not as hungry."

With her attention on the pigeon across the other side of the open space, Vicky took the catapult from Flynn, loaded it with a round stone, and pulled the catapult back. A deep breath did enough to still her aim. With one eye closed, she focused on the fat grey bird and let the catapult go with a *thwack*.

A burst of grey feathers and the pigeon fell on its side.

Vicky jogged across the open space with Flynn behind her. When she got to the bird, she pressed it into the ground with her foot. The thing twitched beneath the pressure. "Put it out of its misery," she said to Flynn.

Although he gulped, Flynn brought his foot up and stamped

on the bird's head. Its small skull crunched beneath his pressure and the creature fell limp.

Vicky lifted the dead bird up by its feet. She retrieved some string from her pocket, bound the creature's legs together, and tied the bird to her belt.

"We'll eat this later." She looked up at the sky. It may have still been warm, but the day wouldn't last forever. "I want to be well away from this place before it gets dark."

Chapter Twenty-Eight

The dead bird slapped against Vicky's right thigh as she walked. About twenty minutes since she'd strapped the thing to her, she barely noticed the repeated pressure now. From the look of the sky, Vicky would have guessed it to be about seven in the evening. Not quite the height of summer, night had started to show signs of settling in as was typical for this time of year. Other than the scuff of their feet over the craggy road and the occasional rustle of long grass, silence surrounded the pair.

Vicky's eyes stung from watching their surroundings; the less she blinked, the less chance she had of missing something. The school had been as she'd predicted: open and easy to spot anyone approaching them. Now they walked down the town's high street, Vicky wound tight in anticipation of an ambush. Regardless of no evidence to back it up, she couldn't shake the feeling they were being watched.

Old shops with large windows—most of them smashed—lined either side of the road. Every building housed a dark shadow that the diseased could hide in should they so desire. As the day went on, the shadows grew even darker. At the same time, the place looked picked cleaner than a carcass in the desert, so maybe the diseased had moved on. Not that she could think like that; complacency led to death in this new world.

The scuff of a shoe over a hard ground called out into the street. Vicky stopped and shot a paranoid glance in the direction she thought the sound had come from.

She didn't say anything to Flynn, but the boy moved closer to her side. If he hadn't heard it too, her reaction would have been enough to spook him.

A few seconds later, it sounded like the slight clearing of a throat from the opposite side of the road. They were surrounded.

Vicky's already dry mouth dried further, and the need to run balled in her calves. At any moment, the town could come to life. It may not be the diseased, but they were clearly in a place that belonged to someone.

To remain frozen to the spot would only make them more vulnerable, so Vicky set off down the high street in the direction they were heading. Maybe whoever watched them would let them through. A woman and a teenage boy posed no threat, right?

With every step down the high street, the darkness of night around the pair seemed to close in—almost as if the place were tightening its grip on them, squeezing them until they couldn't move.

Something shifted in the shadows to Vicky's right—or at least she thought it did. A darkness within the dark seemed to shuffle slightly. Maybe she'd imagined it.

When she glanced up at the fading light in the sky, she tugged on Flynn's sleeve and picked up her pace.

"I don't like it here," Flynn whispered.

At first, Vicky didn't respond. But if they were being watched, to talk to Flynn couldn't give them away any more. "It seems fine to me." The wobble in her voice undermined her words.

"You don't sound like it seems fine to you."

To admit to his observation could be to encourage the people to come out of the shadows. They didn't need to hide if their cover had been blown. "There's a lot of places for people to hide," Vicky said, "so it's understandable that you're imagining things hiding in them. The mind has a way of playing tricks on us."

"But I'm *not* imagining it."

When something clearly shifted in one of the buildings to their right, Vicky grabbed Flynn and led him down an alleyway on the left.

The tight space amplified their footsteps and called out to anyone observing them, but they had to get the fuck off the high street. Maybe whatever lurked there would stay there.

Vicky's pulse ran away on her by the time she'd stepped out of the alleyway and into an old car park. An automobile graveyard, the vehicles sat as exhausted memories of what they once were. Flat tyres had grass growing up the sides of them. Grimy windows collected moss and mould on their perished seals. Rust coated their bodywork like acne.

With more of an open space in front of them, Vicky grabbed Flynn's hand and jogged across the car park with him. As she ran, she checked behind. It seemed clear; maybe their plan had worked.

Once out of the other side of the car park, Vicky led them back toward the high street. If she'd judged it correctly, they'd come out lower down and nearly out of the godforsaken place.

When Vicky checked behind them, ice ran through her veins. Silhouettes crowded the alleyway they'd only just left. Not the silhouettes of the diseased; this mob moved with much less urgency, but came at the pair like a rising tide, confident in their clear advantage over the situation.

When Flynn shrieked out, his voice carried over the car park. "Vicky!"

"I see them," she said through clenched teeth. She lowered her voice. "Once we round this corner, we need to run, okay?"

The boy didn't reply.

To run too early could encourage the mob to give chase. Exhausted from their journey, Vicky had the beating of diseased in her, but real live people, the first she'd seen in a decade, other than those in her party … well, who fucking knew what she could do to avoid this lot.

Despite her urge to sprint, Vicky led Flynn around the corner at the same fast march they currently moved at.

Confident they'd gotten out of the crowd's line of sight, Vicky pulled on Flynn's hand. "Now! Let's go."

The pair moved off at a jog, the sound of their feet slapping against the road. Stealth didn't matter anymore. They'd been seen, and it served no purpose to ignore that fact.

Cars lined the street they ran down. Houses on either side. Grass pushed up through the road. The wind tore down it and howled through every building. But Vicky heard no sound from the mob behind. Maybe they just wanted the pair out. If they kept the pace, they'd be out of the large town in five to ten minutes and on their way.

At the end of the street, they could have gone one of two ways. Right seemed like it would lead them away from the town and toward Home.

Without breaking stride, Vicky led the way out of the road, turned right, and stopped instantly. A second later, Flynn skidded to a halt behind her.

A line of people blocked the road. A scraggly bunch, dressed in rags and filthy from what looked like years' of accumulated dirt, they fixed on Vicky and Flynn with their dark stares. When Vicky looked over her shoulder, she nearly lost the strength in her legs. The crowd from behind had appeared. They moved without urgency because they must have known what lay in wait for the pair up ahead. They'd guided Vicky and Flynn into it.

As the pair stood frozen, Vicky locked eyes on the man at the front of the mob. Sure, the crowd looked wild, but they had nothing on him.

Tall, six feet and two inches at least, the man at the front looked like he weighed less than Flynn. Dressed in trousers, a waistcoat, and nothing else, the man didn't even have shoes on. So gaunt, his skin looked vacuum packed to his skull, the man's eyes nestled in two dark pits on his face. In contrast to the shadow that surrounded them, his piercing blue irises focused on Vicky with laser-like precision. As he lifted his hand to point at the pair, his cracked lips pulled back to reveal his clenched teeth. When he hissed, those around him jumped to life. Their roar damn near deafened Vicky and sent her heart into overdrive. When she looked at Flynn, his face pale and eyes wider than ever, she said, "Run!"

Chapter Twenty-Nine

It felt like being chased by thunder when the crowd behind them sparked into a roaring stampede. The sheer force of their charge robbed some of Vicky's strength and she had to fight her inclination to fall to the ground and curl up into a ball. But she kept on, for Flynn's sake if nothing else.

When she looked across at Flynn, his mouth wide as he fought to breathe, his movement clumsy from exhaustion, she forced her words out. "We can do this. We're going to get out of here. I promise."

Although he shot her a look, he didn't reply.

They rounded a bend and managed to put the crowd out of sight. Even though they couldn't evade the intimidating sound, if they kept this pace, maybe they'd outrun them.

A mangle of about fifteen rusting cars blocked the street to their left, so Vicky led them right instead. Every step felt like it could be the last as her strength ebbed away. The diseased scared her for sure, but she'd gotten well used to them. Having not seen other people for a decade or so, how the fuck should she react? They couldn't stand and fight, but it wouldn't be as easy to outsmart them. They had just one choice; run faster than the people behind them. But as the sound of the crowd drew closer, even that plan seemed flawed.

A glance in the direction of the lowering sun and Vicky could see the way out of the town. Maybe they simply wanted them gone. If they got out, hopefully, that would be enough—hopefully.

Every time Vicky and Flynn came to a junction, either a large sinkhole in the road or a blockage of cars gave them only one choice.

Vicky's rucksack continued to slap against her back, the bruising, a hot swollen mess between her shoulder blades. Her hips hurt worse than before, and her lungs felt ready to burst. But she pushed on.

The next bend saw the street narrow down. Too late to do anything but run into it, Vicky could see they were being funnelled into something. The path had been far too contrived for it to be anything but a trap.

"I don't like this," Flynn called out. He lagged a few metres behind her.

"Me either, buddy, but the only option we have is to run."

Cars, piles of rubble, and lumps of wood and furniture all narrowed the road down as they sprinted up it. The tighter space funnelled the sound of the crowd behind them too, almost as if it concentrated the boom of unintelligible malicious intent.

It got so narrow toward the end of the road, Vicky and Flynn could only just barely run side by side. They'd managed to stay ahead of the mob, but Vicky couldn't ignore the dread that sank deep in her gut. They'd been fucked. Whatever would come next, they'd been well and truly screwed.

At that moment, Vicky lost her feet and flipped upside down. With Flynn by her side, she flew upwards, dragged by a tight rope around her ankles.

As she stared up at her feet, a deep pain in her neck, and with Flynn beside her, Vicky fought for breath and yelled, "Fuck!"

About two metres from the ground, the pair swung in the breeze. The ropes around their ankles creaked under the strain of their weight. The traps stank of rot and shit. Not the first things to be caught in them, maybe they were the first things in a long time that weren't infected. And who could blame these people? Maybe they had the entire city set up to trap and execute the diseased. Maybe they'd take it easy on Vicky and Flynn when they realised they hadn't been bitten.

As the crowd caught up with them and gathered around the bottom of the trap, Vicky looked down at the fixed scowls and trembled. Maybe not.

***

After a few minutes, the tall man in the leather waistcoat caught up with the pack and stared up at Vicky and Flynn. When he made eye contact with Vicky, he glared straight into her. It snapped a chill through her frame.

The man bared his teeth again and pointed up. He hissed, loud and prolonged, and all of those surrounding him joined in. The crowd had started at about fifteen strong, but it had near doubled as those at the back caught up.

The man continued to stare up at Vicky and Flynn, but he pointed at a woman with an axe. The axe wielder nodded and swung it at the rope attached to a pulley that had been drilled into a nearby wall.

Vicky's stomach rushed into her feet, and Flynn yipped as they hurtled toward the ground. The hard contact drove the wind from Vicky's body and a nauseating *crack* seemed to realign her entire skeleton.

Flynn vocalised Vicky's pain as he rolled around on the ground and moaned.

Before Vicky had time to catch her breath, the mob wrapped a net around her and Flynn and moved off, dragging the pair behind them. The netting rushed over the hard and broken ground with a *whoosh*.

Flynn squirmed until he'd pulled himself up next to Vicky. "I'm scared."

What could she say to that? Vicky hugged him close to her and looked up. Behind them, staring down with what looked like simmering rage, the tall and gaunt man fixed on the pair.

"I'm scared, too, mate," Vicky whispered as she held Flynn close. "I'm scared, too."

Chapter Thirty

Vicky didn't want to be in the shopping mall, but the smoother floor came as a welcome relief to the cracked concrete they'd been dragged over for the past twenty minutes or so.

The tall and gaunt man continued to walk behind them. So withdrawn, his face looked like a bird's skull, he no longer looked down at them. Instead, he stared directly ahead and marched. A sergeant major in the power he exuded, the rest of his gang responded to his silent authority, often looking back at him as if to make sure they'd read his mood right. The man clearly put everyone on edge.

When they got to a shop, the rush of the lifting shutters at the front called out through the abandoned mall. Three men dragged Vicky and Flynn into the middle of the space, pulled the nets off them, took their rucksacks and weapons, and left them in the shop.

The shutter rattled as they dragged it to the floor with a loud *crash*!

The floor may have been hard and cold, but at least Vicky could stretch out. She pushed her fingers and toes in as far opposing directions as she could manage. Nowhere near banishing all her aches and pains, she found some relief in the gesture and got to her feet.

When Flynn got up beside her, Vicky looked around the dark space. The light came from the main area of the shopping mall, which lit up the front of the shop, but cast the back in dark shadow. When Vicky heard the whimper of someone in the darkness, her heart raced, and she pulled Flynn behind her.

The first fear that they shared the space with a diseased vanished almost instantly. The diseased didn't snivel and cry when they saw a human; they roared with all they had and came forward like a steam train.

The guards had taken most things from Vicky, but they'd failed to find her flint. When she stepped closer into the shadows, she pulled the item from her pocket, checked to see that no one outside paid her much interest, and sparked it.

The magnesium flash lit up the man in the corner. He had a long beard and scraggly hair. He looked like he'd been there a long time as he huddled with his knees pulled into his chest, shook his head, and cried.

Vicky sparked the flint again and got a glimpse of his bloodshot eyes. Confused and distressed, the man seemed lost as he glared up at her. The flash had shown Vicky that the rest of the shop sat empty.

As she walked closer to the man at the back, the smell of piss ran up her nostrils, and she twisted her face against its ammonia reek. "Excuse me, are you okay?" Not that she cared; she had her own shit to deal with. What she should have said is, "will you harm us?" but that wouldn't go down well.

The man made more noise as he whimpered and cried.

Before Vicky could say anything, he spoke. "Take me. They take me. Burn. Feed. Hungry. Dry. Cold. Take me. Can't. Just can't." When he let out a shrill scream, Vicky's heart damn near exploded, and she jumped backwards, clattering into Flynn behind her.

The closer she'd gotten to the man, the more distressed he'd seemed, so Vicky took Flynn's hand and led him back toward the shutters that faced out into the mall.

The guard on the shutter didn't seem like the rest of them. A woman in her forties, she had long blonde hair that looked like it had been cleaned recently. She had kind features.

The shutter bowed outwards at the pressure Vicky put on it, and it felt cold against her face when she leaned toward the woman. "Excuse me," she said, "can you please tell me what's going on here?"

Although the woman didn't reply, Vicky saw her flinch.

Before Vicky could ask anything else, the scream of a diseased ripped through the mall, followed by the crash as it hit the shutter of the shop opposite her. The monster fell backwards from where it collided with the shutter before it jumped to its feet again and pressed its face against the bars.

Flynn pressed into Vicky's side, and she felt him shiver next to her.

"What the fuck?" Vicky said to the woman. "Why are you keeping diseased here?"

The woman still didn't reply, but she looked like she wanted to.

"Okay," Vicky said, "I'm obviously asking the wrong questions. Let me try again. Do you know anything about Home?"

The woman looked over this time.

"Come on, please tell me. Flynn and I plan to go there, and we want to know if it's a trap or not." Not that she needed to concern herself with another trap. They needed to get out of their current one first.

Although she looked ahead as if to ignore the pair, the woman spoke from the side of her mouth. "We've seen the signposts for Home."

"It's well signposted, is it?" Flynn asked.

"Sure, once you get out of the city."

Flynn tried to speak again, but Vicky put a hand on his shoulder to stop him. They didn't need the woman clamming up from too many questions. "And why aren't you there? What's wrong with them?"

When the woman turned to look at Vicky, sadness glistened in her eyes.

With the gap too small for her head, Vicky stretched her hand through the cold metal bars instead and touched the woman's forearm. "Come on, love, you can tell us. Please?"

Darkness swept across the woman's features, and she screwed her face up when she said, "Let's just say they have different tastes than us, shall we?"

"What does that mean?"

But Vicky had lost her at that point. The woman clearly had no interest in continuing the conversation, and she pulled her arm away from Vicky.

"Come on, Flynn," Vicky said as she led the boy away from the shutter and retreated into the shadows in the corner opposite the whimpering man.

***

It could have been minutes, it could have been hours, but eventually the tall and gaunt man arrived at the front of the shop. Without a word, he flicked his head at one of the guards he'd brought with him, who opened the shutters. The loud metal barrier clattered on its runners as the man lifted it all the way open and stepped inside.

With a torch as big as his face, the guard lit the place up and temporarily blinded Vicky. She flinched away from the strong beam, and before she'd regained her sight, the man had grabbed Flynn.

"Vicky," he cried as he shook and twisted. "Vicky, help me, please."

As Vicky made to stand up, the tall and gaunt man said the first word she'd heard him speak. It came out as a deep boom like a cannon had been fired in the enclosed space. "NO!"

The guard instantly let go of Flynn, and Vicky couldn't blame him. She'd never seen anyone with the authority of this man. When he spoke—which clearly didn't happen very often—people listened.

The tall man then pointed at the whimpering mess in the corner.

The guard walked over to the other man and grabbed his foot. When he yanked it backwards, the man in the corner fell and whacked his head against the hard floor with a loud and hollow *tonk*.

Although the man twisted and turned, screamed and wailed, the guard continued to drag him away. In such a state Vicky couldn't make out a single word he said, she watched the distressed man leave their lives.

The second he'd crossed the shop's threshold, the woman guard pulled the shutters down and bolted them to the floor again.

Vicky got to her feet and pulled Flynn in close to her. He shook and cried in her arms. She hugged him tight as she watched the man and his gang drag the distressed prisoner off.

Once they'd moved far enough away from the shop, Vicky walked back toward the front near the shutters and looked out. She had a clear view of the centrepiece of the shopping centre. It looked like it had been a water feature of some sort in the past—maybe a fountain or something—but now it had been made into a fire pit.

As they got the distressed man closer, he kicked and screamed and fought against his captors. The closer they got to the fire pit, the more vehement his protest.

Once at the pit, several other gang members appeared and held the man upright and still. One of the gang grabbed his hair and pulled back so he faced the ceiling.

The tall and gaunt man marched up to him, a long curved blade in his hand. He looked at the distressed man before he leaned in close and sniffed him.

The back of Vicky's knees turned weak.

The tall and gaunt man then brought his knife up to their prisoner's throat. The prisoner screamed louder than before, and it set off the diseased person in the shop opposite them.

Before Vicky could grab Flynn and cover his eyes, the tall and gaunt man had ripped the blade across his prisoner's throat.

Blood shot forward from the prisoner, and the tall and gaunt man leaned into the flow with his mouth open wide. When he pulled away, blood coated his face and chest. He smiled a skeletal grin and pointed at the fire pit.

***

The process seemed to last an age, but they finally had the dead prisoner tied to a spit above the fire. More wood had been dragged onto the blaze and the flames rose up. When the fire caught his blood-soaked skin, the dead man sizzled.

The acrid reek of charred pork reached Vicky, and she heaved. A glance at Flynn, and she saw the twisted distaste on his features.

They hadn't said anything to one another for the entire time. Flynn finally turned to Vicky, a warble in his voice. "We need to get the fuck out of here. Now!"

Chapter Thirty-One

The shadows at the back of their prison called to Vicky. If she withdrew into them, she wouldn't be able to see the cooking man. Maybe if she stepped those few metres farther back, she also wouldn't have to endure the charred reek of his skin. But she remained by the shutter, not to watch the vile ritual out in the mall, but rather to watch the woman who stood on guard by their shop. A grimace of discomfort had sat on her face with every painful second of the murder and bizarre spit roast. As much as she tried to act the part, this woman didn't belong here.

Vicky moved closer to the woman and spoke so only she would hear. "You're not into this are you?"

As the woman stared straight ahead, a twitch ran through her stony expression.

Vicky spoke in a soft voice. "It's okay, I know you're not like *them*. I can see you have some humanity left."

Still no reply, but Vicky saw a tear run down the woman's face.

"What are you doing here?"

After a deep breath, the woman continued to stare ahead and

spoke quietly. "I came here because I needed to survive and they offered shelter."

"That makes sense."

"They eat the diseased," the woman said.

The comment ran ice through Vicky, and she lost her words for a moment. After a deep breath, she finally said, "*What?*"

"I know," the woman replied, "fucked up, right?"

When Vicky looked at Flynn, she saw the shock on his face, but he didn't speak. "How have you avoided getting infected?"

"They boil the meat for so long it seems to kill the virus. As gross as it is, it works. I'm prepared to eat it to survive. They're not human anymore."

Vicky nodded but didn't respond as the bitter taste of bile lifted up into her throat. Just the thought of it … she'd rather die than eat diseased human meat.

"But we have some people here, like Zander—"

"Zander?"

"The creepy guy with the knife. He's clearly always craved human flesh. You take away rules from society, and it seems like an open invite to the perverts, freaks, and nutters. When the chips are down, a lot of people will do what they need to do to survive. People like Zander, however, seem to positively thrive from the change of status quo."

As the woman spoke, Vicky looked over at the tall and gaunt man. A chill ripped through her to watch him. He stood perfectly still with his hands clasped together in front of him and stared at the cooking man.

Before Vicky could ask the woman anything more, the scream of another diseased called out in the shopping mall. The hard floor and closed off shops created a huge echo chamber that amplified its tormented yell.

Several people appeared with a diseased in their grip. Two men held an arm of the monster each and a woman held it around the neck. The diseased had been a man in its previous incarnation, a large man. Although outnumbered three to one, the diseased put up a good fight as it twisted and bit at the air around it.

Vicky watched her guard put her hand in her pocket and pull a key out. She then walked over to the shop opposite—the one with the diseased in it—and bent down to undo the padlock at the bottom. Although dark, Vicky saw the shadows shift as the diseased within the shop rushed forward. The woman snapped her hand away from the lock as the diseased hit the metal shutter with a loud *crash*.

For the briefest second, the guard looked at her hand, checked around, and then looked over at the three people coming her way with their newly caught diseased.

Another woman had joined the two men and woman as they brought the diseased over. With a long spear in her hand, she walked toward the shutter that held the first diseased back, and stabbed it through the gap in the bars. The diseased roared and jumped backwards.

In one fluid movement, the woman who had guarded Vicky and Flynn, pulled the shutters up. The diseased inside the shop roared again and rushed forward, but the woman with the spear stabbed it for a second time. It retreated back into the darkness and screamed from the shadows.

Clearly well-practiced, the three people shoved the new

diseased forward, tripping it as they forced it into the shop, and dragged the shutter back down again with a loud *boom*.

Vicky's guard slipped the padlock around the bottom of the shutter and snapped it into place before she stepped back and looked at the other people who'd helped contain the new diseased. All five of them panted from the effort, and then backed away without a word.

When the guard returned to Vicky's cage, she wore a pained frown and held one of her hands with the other one. Vicky glanced down, and despite the darkness of their surroundings, she saw the blood glisten on her hand. The air left her lungs, and she spoke in no more than a whisper. "You've been bitten."

The woman frowned at Vicky. "Shut the fuck up."

"But you've been *bitten*."

The woman turned on Vicky. Malice gripped her features as she scowled at her. "Do you want me to tell Zander you're causing trouble?"

Vicky didn't reply. Instead, she stared at the woman and the sweat that had already beaded on her brow. As she backed away, she pulled Flynn with her.

Chapter Thirty-Two

Vicky pulled Flynn far enough back in the cell so their guard wouldn't feel pressured, but not so far back that she could forget about them, and watched on. What could she do? If she called to the others that the guard had been bitten, the guard would be taken out, and a new one would be instated to watch them. Although, should the woman change and infect the others, they could be stuck in the cell indefinitely. But maybe with everyone gone, they'd at least be able to make some noise in trying to escape. There had to be a way out—an air vent, or something like that. If the diseased ripped through this community, it would rid the world of a band of cannibals. That in itself had to be worth keeping her mouth shut for.

With Flynn so close he pressed into her side, Vicky watched sweat pour down the guard's face. The woman wiped her blonde fringe away from her forehead, but the second she let it go, her fine hair fell again and stuck to her skin.

As the woman pulled at her collar, Vicky stepped forward a pace. Fuck knows why, but she could see this woman needed something. Comfort if nothing else. "How are you feeling?"

The woman growled as if fighting the disease's possession of her. "How the fuck do you think I'm feeling?"

"Thank you for being kind to us."

The woman spun around, her eyes rolling in her head as she tried to focus on Vicky. "I've not been kind to you."

"You could have been worse. I can see you're not like them." When Vicky looked at the gathered crowd by the cooking man, she saw their clear excitement in their agitation. It looked like a fight could break out at any moment if they didn't get fed.

A few seconds passed where the woman didn't respond. Instead, she stared out into the mall and rode what seemed like waves of pain, her teeth clenched and her breaths heavy. With a trembling hand, she reached into her trouser pocket and pulled a key out. She held it behind her so Vicky could take it and spoke in a whisper. "Just wait for everything to change before you try to leave, okay?"

As Vicky stepped forward, she drew a dry gulp. "Thank you."

With the same subtlety she'd used with the key, the woman continued to look ahead and passed a small bottle of water behind her through the gap in the bars. "Fresh water too. The seal's not been broken, so you don't have to worry about me poisoning you."

"I didn't think you would."

"Well, you *should*. You shouldn't trust anyone." All the while, the woman stared straight ahead at the excited pack of cannibals.

Vicky remained quiet.

The guard's face twisted. "I had a son about the same age as your boy when the virus happened. He must have been about eight when it all kicked off, right?"

"Six."

The woman drew a deep breath. "I watched him get torn apart in front of me. It killed me; deadened me inside. I wandered for so long after that before I fell in with this lot. But I'm not like them, and thank you for reminding me of that."

A nod and Vicky said, "You're welcome."

As the woman remained rigid at the front of the shop—her shoulders pulled back, her chin raised—blood leaked from her eyes. In just a few seconds, the kindness left her soft face, and she scowled against what must have been the pain of changing.

"What's your name?" Vicky asked.

The woman snapped her head round, and a small amount of blood fell to the floor. "Huh?"

The sight of the woman—her face striped red with her bloody tears—forced Vicky back a pace. "Uh, your name, love? What name can I remember you by?"

What seemed to be the last bit of humanity remaining in the woman stared out from her bleeding eyes. "Amelia," she said. "My name's Amelia."

"Thank you, Amelia." With the key in her pocket and the bottle of water in her hand, Vicky withdrew into the shadows and pulled Flynn with her.

When her back hit the cold wall at the rear of the shop, she waited. A second later and a spasm twitched through Amelia that threw her right arm out and away from her body. She bent forward at the waist and rested her hands on her knees. A couple of deep breaths later and she released a low growl. When she stood up again, her form had twisted like every diseased Vicky had seen since the outbreak.

The woman then turned around and looked into the shop. The confusion on her face suggested she had some recollection of the people inside, but she couldn't see them. She scanned the place, her head movements twitchy, her mouth hung loose.

When Vicky felt Flynn press into her side again, she put an arm around him and spoke in a whisper. "It's okay; she can't see us."

"How do you—?" but before Flynn could finish his question, the woman spun on her heel and sprinted off. She headed directly for the cooking man and all of the people around the fire waiting for him to be done. With their attention so fixed on their meal, none of them seemed to see what bore down on them.

Chapter Thirty-Three

Although hunger gnawed away at Vicky, at least the woman's water had quenched her thirst. It hadn't completely satiated it, but it had taken the edge off. She'd given Flynn as much as she'd taken herself, so hopefully he felt some relief too.

The pair had slid down to the floor, the hard and cold ground turning Vicky's arse numb, but it relieved the ache in her legs. About twenty minutes had passed. During that time, they'd watched the woman rush over to the first person by the fire and bite her. She moved on and got three other people before the cannibals had realised what had hit them. In the chaos that erupted, Amelia got several more bites in. By the time the gang had taken her down, the others had turned. At least eight diseased at that point; they overwhelmed the rest of the gang.

With the man on the spit untended, the smell of charred pork turned into thick smoke that caught in Vicky's throat. The need to cough balled in her oesophagus, but she managed to hold it back. The diseased didn't need to know they were there.

When one of the diseased ran straight into the shutters in front of them with a loud *crash*, Vicky jumped, making it worse for Flynn's startled jolt next to her. The diseased man paced up and down outside the shop and looked into the darkness. He clearly knew that the shop held something of interest, but he didn't seem able to grasp exactly what that was.

What felt like an age passed before the diseased man finally ran off again.

While the screams of the diseased echoed throughout the shopping mall, Vicky didn't speak to Flynn. Instead, she wrapped an arm around him and pulled him in close her.

***

A few hours later, and with aches running from her bottom all the way up her back and through her shoulders, Vicky pulled away from Flynn. They hadn't seen anyone for some time, so she leaned close to him and finally spoke. "You stay here. I'm going to check what's happening out there. We may be able to leave now."

Grit crunched beneath Vicky's footsteps as she walked over the hard floor toward the closed shutter. Dirt had always coated the shop's floor, but Vicky became much more aware of it because of the silence now outside. With her eyes spread so wide they stung, she did all she could to see into the dark mall beyond. Night had well and truly settled in, but the strong moon shone through the glass ceiling and lit the place up.

Just a metre from the shutter and a *crash* exploded through it. As Vicky jumped backwards, her heart rate on overdrive, she tripped and landed on her arse. The jolt from the hard floor ran from her coccyx to the base of her neck and forced stars into her vision.

As she sat up, she looked at the large diseased man in front of her. The tall and gaunt figure—their leader, Zander—pressed against the shutters. The shutter bowed in against his pressure. Hollow cheeks, sunken eyes, long features, bloodstained skin, the man fixed his hunger—or lust, or whatever the fuck it was—on Vicky. She found him less intimidating now he'd changed, somehow less of a monster.

Despite the pain in her back, Vicky pushed off against the floor and shifted toward Flynn.

As she got farther into the shop and the protective umbrella of the shadows, she watched the fury on Zander's face dilute. From his reaction, she saw exactly when she'd become invisible to him.

When she got close to Flynn, she reached out and hugged him again. "It looks quieter out there."

"So what do we do?"

It would have been sensible to try to get some sleep, especially as Vicky hadn't had any over the past few days, but she couldn't relax enough to sleep. No matter how her body ached, she had to watch the outside of the shop.

"We wait until morning and judge the situation then."

Chapter Thirty-Four

At some point, Vicky must have fallen asleep, because when she woke, it had gotten light outside.

Flynn still slept next to her, his head against her breast. He'd be so embarrassed to know he'd used her right tit as a pillow all night. She'd make sure she told him one day.

Before Flynn woke, Vicky moved away from him. As she pushed him upright, he opened his eyes and blinked away his sleep. "Huh?" he said.

"It's morning, Flynn."

He stretched up to the ceiling and twisted his face from the effort of it. Lucidity spread across his features, and he stared at the shutter. "They're gone now, are they?"

"I don't know. I haven't seen anything move in a while."

"Were you asleep too?"

Vicky shrugged. "Yeah, but I think I would have heard them and woken up."

Although he didn't reply, Flynn gave Vicky a skeptical look.

"I think we need to at least see what's going on out there now," Vicky said. "Most of them have probably fucked off. You know what the diseased are like; if they can't see food, they move on. They only stayed at the containers because of all the noise we made."

Vicky got to her feet and held her hand out to Flynn. The boy took it and stood up. They continued to hold hands and Vicky looked into his eyes. "I think we'll be okay. Once we're out of here, we can get out of the city and find Home."

Flynn nodded at her.

The pair walked over to the shutters and peered out. "It seems abandoned," Vicky said as she squinted against the bright sun that shone through the glass ceiling. The sunshine lit up the charred man on the spit, who smoked where he lay, the fire beneath him aglow with hot embers.

Vicky crouched down and put her hand through the bars to reach the padlock. Panic accelerated through her to have her hand outside of the shop; anything could grab it at any point. As she lifted the bottom of the large brass lock to face her, she slipped the key from her pocket. She shook as she pinched the small silver object.

"Are you sure we should do this? If we open that shutter, we could be inviting in God knows what."

"I think the diseased have moved on."

"Think?"

"What do you want from me, Flynn? We can't stay in here forever."

Vicky stared at Flynn for a few seconds. When he didn't reply, she returned her attention to the shutter and did her best to still her pounding heart.

Painfully aware of Flynn's focus on her, Vicky pressed the

key into the lock. Or at least, that's what she'd planned to do. As she applied pressure to the key, it hadn't quite found the hole. She'd expected it to slide in, but instead, it popped away from the lock and pinged out into the mall.

As it skittered across the floor away from them, Vicky's heart sank, and nausea lurched through her as she withdrew from the shutter and sat down. "Fuck."

Chapter Thirty-Five

"Why do you have to breathe down my neck the entire time?" Vicky looked up at Flynn. "Well?"

"Um ... I, um ..."

"*I, um* isn't an answer, Flynn. I've been protecting you for most of your life, and you start to question my decisions now? Jesus, what's wrong with you?"

Instead of a response, Flynn stared at Vicky and his mouth hung loose.

In that moment, Vicky saw his dad; the Rhys that she'd rescued at the water fountain in Summit City. "I should have carried on running."

"Huh?" Flynn said, his eyes glazed with tears.

Vicky shook her head and turned her back on him. Utter despondency pulled on her frame when she looked at the key about a metre away from her. In the middle of the mall's walkway, she had no fucking chance of getting it. No fucking chance.

After a deep sigh, she slumped where she sat. She kept her focus on the key and softened her tone. "I'm sorry, mate; I've fucked up."

Flynn sat down next to her and stared out at the key. The bright sun from the glass ceiling glistened off the small silver object as if to taunt their failed attempt at freedom.

Before either of them spoke again, Flynn got to his feet. Vicky watched him walk to the back of the shop and disappear into the shadows. A few seconds later, he returned with the empty water bottle they'd drunk from; the one given to them by Amelia.

Flynn looked like he had a plan, so Vicky said nothing as she watched him.

First, he removed the lid from the empty container. He then bit into the side of the bottle, which made a loud crunch of plastic that called through the deserted mall.

Despite her urge to tell him to be quiet, Vicky said nothing, tensed up and looked out into the shopping centre. It seemed clear, and even if it wasn't, it hardly mattered now; they'd starve to death in the cage if they didn't get out. Besides, if any diseased saw them, they wouldn't be able to get through the shutter anyway.

Hopelessness weighted Vicky's heart as she watched the boy bite the bottle with the side of his mouth. He looked like a dog. Each crunch ran through the shopping mall and lifted her tense shoulders to her neck. Just before Vicky told him to shut the fuck up, Flynn stopped and pulled the bottle away.

The same crackle of plastic sounded out when he dug his finger into the hole he'd made. After he'd wiggled it around for a few seconds, he pulled the hole bigger until he'd separated the top half of the bottle from the bottom.

"What are you doing?" Vicky asked, but Flynn didn't reply.

Instead, he slipped his shoes off and removed the laces. He tied them together and then threaded the lace in through the bottle neck before he dropped it out of the large hole at the bottom. He then tied it along the side of the plastic container.

For the first time since he'd sat down to make his contraption, he looked over at Vicky and pulled a tense smile. When he stood up, he pressed his face to the shop's shutters and stared out into the mall. Vicky did the same; it seemed empty.

Louder than even the construction of his implement, the shutters rattled when Flynn leaned against them. With the bottle still in his hand, he shoved his arm through a gap all the way up to his shoulder. He seemed more focused on the bottle than on the potential danger of a diseased. Vicky watched the mall beyond them. Let him focus on his task; she'd drag him back if she needed to.

With half of her attention on Flynn, Vicky saw him swing the bottle at the end of the shoelace from side to side. Flynn built up a good swing with the pendulum before he grunted and changed the direction to thrust the bottle out toward the key on the floor.

The shutters rattled from where he lurched forward, and the half a bottle hit the hard floor with a *crack*. It missed the key.

As Flynn reeled it back in, Vicky leaned close to him. "Try to keep the noise down. We don't know what's out there still, and we don't want to make too much of a commotion."

But the boy ignored her. And rightly so. Noise and a key beat silence and starving to death in their prison.

The swinging bottle mesmerised Vicky. She shook her head to pull herself from the hypnotic daze. The shopping mall, empty and bright beyond their prison, still seemed abandoned. Although, *seemed* meant fuck all when you had to bet a life on it.

When Flynn grunted again as he launched the bottle, Vicky watched it land over the key. With her heart in her throat, she observed as he gently pulled on the shoelace. Because of the way he'd tied it, the bottle remained upright as he dragged it, and it brought the key back with it.

Patient beyond his years, Flynn pulled the bottle in an inch at a time and Vicky couldn't help but smile. Maybe she needed to give him more credit.

With the key no more than two feet away, Flynn dropped to the floor and stretched his arm out. He pushed out so the bars ran up to his shoulder again.

Vicky watched him find millimetres more stretch as he got closer to the key.

When he finally touched the metal object, she jumped for joy and landed with a thud. But the thud hadn't come from her. A glance to her right and Vicky saw it. About three metres from them, a diseased child of no more than about eight ran at them. Silent at first, when the girl locked eyes on Vicky, she screamed like a harpy.

Chapter Thirty-Six

In one fluid movement, Vicky jumped back, grabbed Flynn by his ankles, and yanked him backwards. The cage shook as she pulled with all of her might and Flynn's arm dragged through the bars.

The second Vicky had pulled Flynn away, the girl crashed down where his hand had been. She landed face first, her misplaced bite connecting with the hard floor rather than the back of Flynn's hand. The thud of her fall shook the shutter, and she fell limp as she crashed into it with a clatter.

When they heard the cries of more diseased, their shrill call echoing throughout the abandoned mall, Vicky and Flynn retreated into the shadows at the back of the shop.

Once cloaked in darkness, Vicky breathed heavily from the adrenaline rush and leaned so close to Flynn she could smell the dirt on him. "Did you get it?"

He shook in response.

"I can't see what you're doing with your head."

When Vicky felt his hand touch hers, she opened her grip. Flynn pressed the small metal object into her palm.

Vicky put her arm around him and pulled him close. "Well done, mate. Well done."

A second later, three more diseased ran up to the shop's shutters. They looked down at the unconscious girl before they peered into the space beyond. Although Vicky knew they couldn't see her, she couldn't control her frantic pulse. To be the focus of the things' bloody eyes when they stood just metres away triggered something in her—a natural shot of adrenaline that told her to get the fuck out. Most of the time that's exactly what she'd do. But since they'd been locked in the shop, they'd have to grimace and bear it.

***

At a guess, Vicky would have said two hours had passed since they'd seen a diseased outside the shop. She patted Flynn's shoulder as she stood up. "At some point, we're going to have to move on, mate."

Flynn followed Vicky's lead and got to his feet. Since he'd put the key in her hand, Vicky had gripped it so tightly her palm sweated. However, as they got closer to the shutter, she handed it back to Flynn. "I think you've proven you have a much steadier hand than I do."

Visibly inflated by the comment, Flynn took the key from Vicky and nodded at her.

Vicky kept lookout again as Flynn reached through the bars and undid the padlock. He did it with ease. If she'd have just let him do it in the first place, then maybe they'd be long gone by now.

Together they slowly lifted the shutter. Although it made

some sound, the diseased would have to be close to hear it.

Once outside the shop in the huge open space of the shopping mall, Vicky looked around and drew a dry gulp. Smoke hung in the air still from the burned man above the fire pit. It would have been best to avoid the hideous sight completely, but when Vicky saw her telescopic baton and Flynn's baseball bat near the burned man, her shoulders slumped. They couldn't leave their weapons behind.

"Don't look, Flynn," Vicky said as she walked over and retrieved both her baton and Flynn's bat. She also found the catapult, a spear, and a large machete. Although she'd told Flynn not to look, she couldn't help but stare at the burned man on the spit herself. Black and hard like an old lump of wood, he still retained his human form. Maybe the man would turn to ash at some point and join the rest of it in the fire pit. Vicky screwed her nose up at the charred stench and pulled on Flynn's arm. "Come on, mate, let's go."

The boy had been frozen to the spot as he stared at the burned corpse, and Vicky's tug barely registered with him. When she looked closer, she saw where he had his attention. The remains of his rucksack smouldered in the fire pit. Another tug, more gentle this time, and Flynn came with her.

They walked away from the mall and the fire pit with their weapons raised and ready to use.

***

When Vicky stepped out of the front of the mall, the city awash with the green of nature, and the sun warm on her face, she drew a deep breath of the fresh air. It went some way to clearing the stench of the burned man, although she'd smell the memory of him for a lifetime.

After she'd patted Flynn on the back, she said, "Let's get the fuck out of this horrible town."

Chapter Thirty-Seven

A few days without food sapped Vicky's energy, but she pushed on. Lighter because of no rucksack, she negotiated the overgrown streets with Flynn by her side. Were it not for him, they'd still be in that bloody shop as they contemplated starving to death.

When they reached a high spot in the town, Vicky placed her hands on her hips and drew deep breaths as she looked out at the road that led away from the place. "Not long now and we'll be out of here. I can't wait to get to Home."

After he'd wrung his hands for a few seconds, Flynn said, "What do you think Amelia meant when she said that Home don't have the same tastes as them?"

"That they don't eat people, mate. Diseased or otherwise." For all the maturity the boy had shown, his childish naivety still shone through.

"Ever since I heard the first broadcast from the place," Vicky said, "I've had a good feeling about it. Life will change for the better when we get there."

Flynn stared at her and gulped, so Vicky put an arm around

his shoulders. "And if it doesn't, then we'll find somewhere else."

***

As they ran down the other side of the large hill, sweat rolled down Vicky's face. The road—cracked and sprouting grass—ran a heavy jolt through her body every time one of her feet hit the ground.

A more modern part of the large town, Vicky looked at the houses on either side of the road. They'd clearly been thrown up quickly and with little thought about appearance. They looked like they'd all been designed from the same plans. Nature had taken a bigger bite from them than it had some of the older houses. Vines and weeds blew out what seemed to be cheap walls, and many of them had huge holes in the sides of them.

Most houses had a driveway with one car or another. It seemed like every other house had a rusty old four-by-four. Vicky smiled as she passed the status symbols. The ridiculous cars meant fuck all now.

***

"Vicky," Flynn said, and Vicky stopped running. Something about his hushed tone stopped her dead.

"Look."

A fox stood at the side of the road with its snout in a mound of earth.

Vicky held her hand out, and Flynn passed her the catapult. Not the time for training, they needed to eat and couldn't afford for him to miss.

With the weapon in her grip, Vicky loaded it with one of the round stones she kept in her pocket, pulled it back, and released it.

As always, the stone nailed the skinny canid, and it fell on its side.

Flynn rushed past Vicky with his bat raised and skulled the fox before it could recover. When he lifted it up, the creature hung limp from his grip.

The town seemed deserted, so Vicky pointed at one of the cheap houses on the side of the road. "I know we said we'd get out of this place, but I think we should eat first."

With eyes like saucers, Flynn looked at the fox like he'd eat it raw.

Vicky laughed. "I'll take that as you agreeing with me then, shall I?"

***

After Vicky and Flynn had cooked and eaten the fox, they returned to the open road. Far from a pleasant experience, the fox tasted rich and gamey, and they had to eat it so quickly it gave Vicky indigestion. But nothing had bothered them while they'd eaten, so the pair moved off again at a fast walk.

Not a lot mattered now other than survival, so Vicky put her attention on the shadows that surrounded them. Narrow alleyways, dark windows in the houses, the occasional newsagents—hell, even the ridiculous cars could have something lurking inside of them. They'd been lucky to eat without any interruption. That luck had to run out at some point.

At the bottom of the hill, Vicky finally saw the way out of the town. The exit road stretched wide enough for three lanes on either side, and fields flanked it.

***

Once they'd left the town, Vicky paused to catch her breath. They'd only moved at a fast walk, but she still felt exhausted. The recently eaten fox sat as a lump in her stomach. As she looked at the place they'd left behind, she said, "More like a city, really."

Flynn glanced back at the place but didn't reply. And why would he? She'd had most of the conversation in her head. "The town's more like a city than a town," she explained, before adding, "I thought we were going to get jumped by something on the way out."

"We were lucky we didn't," Flynn replied. "We really tempted fate by stopping to eat."

Before Vicky could say anything else, Flynn drew a deep breath that lifted his chest and screwed his face up at her. "I'm not as useless as you think, you know?"

Vicky reached out and touched his arm. "Where's this come from?" She walked off and pulled him with her so they could get away from the town.

"I wanted to say something earlier," Flynn said, "but we had too much going on in the town."

"Besides," Vicky said, "who said you were useless?"

"You didn't need to say it. You've treated me like a fucking child ever since Mum and Dad died. *You* were the one who said I should be allowed to grow up, but you're worse than they were.

I only got us out of that shop because you couldn't prevent me from taking action."

"I'm sorry you feel that way, Flynn."

"Don't be sorry, just treat me like an adult." When he looked down at the ground, his bottom lip poked out. "I'm not useless."

Other than the wind through the long grass and the scuff of their feet over the hard ground, silence hung between the pair. When Vicky drew a breath to speak, Flynn looked across at her and squinted because of the sun.

"I struggle to trust anyone to do anything," Vicky said. "It's not because I think you're a child. It's just"—she sighed— "well, I had a horrible home life after my dad died and was treated like an arsehole by my mum and brothers for years. I then met Brendan, who, as you know, is the reason the world's fucked. I dunno, I've kind of lost my faith in people. I figure that if I do it all on my own, then I don't have to rely on anyone else."

When she looked back at Flynn, she saw him continue to watch her as he walked, but he didn't speak.

"All I can do," she continued, "is promise you that I'll treat you like an adult. To do what I tried to force your parents to do."

After a curt nod, Flynn forced a smile. "Thank you."

Although Vicky glanced behind several times as they walked, she didn't see any diseased burst from the large town.

The grass on either side of the road stood at about chest height on Vicky, and the large tufts that sprouted through the asphalt dragged on her feet. At different points, grass covered the entire road.

"They burned our bags," Flynn finally said.

"Huh?"

"Our rucksacks …"

"Yeah."

"I had a few bits left to remind me of Mum and Dad in there."

"I'm sorry, mate," Vicky said because she had nothing else. "I'm truly sorry."

Flynn shrugged and dragged his feet as they continued to walk away from the hellish labyrinth of a town.

Chapter Thirty-Eight

"What's that?" Flynn said as they ran.

When Vicky looked to where Flynn had pointed, she just made it out. A white baton of wood—or at least partly white; most of the paint had blistered and come away from it. It poked just above the long grass.

The pair looked at one another before they left the road and ran toward it.

When they got close enough, they saw the sign clearly. At least three feet deep and a couple of feet wide, instructions had been painted on it in red — *YOU'RE JUST ONE HOUR'S WALK FROM HOME. ALL ARE WELCOME. WE HAVE FOOD AND SHELTER. ALL WE ASK IS THAT YOU SHARE OUR COMMON GOAL OF DEFEATING THE DISEASED. AND THAT YOU COME WITH PEACE IN YOUR HEART. IF YOU WANT THAT, WE WILL ACCEPT YOUR HELP IN ANY WAY YOU CAN GIVE IT.*

After she'd read the words, Vicky looked at Flynn, his mouth moving slightly as he finished reading the sign too.

For the first time in days, Vicky saw hope on the boy's face, and the child she'd help raise returned with his excitement when he said, "We're not far now."

"I know. Now we're out of that city, we have the hard bit behind us. We have hours of daylight left and only need an hour to get there. I knew we'd find it; I just knew it. I can't wait to sleep in a—"

Vicky didn't finish her sentence. The shrill cry of what sounded like hundreds of diseased, and the stampede of their heavy feet, cut her short. When she looked in the direction of the sound, her heart sank. It came from the direction they needed to travel in to get to Home.

Chapter Thirty-Nine

An old brick farmhouse poked out of the field about five hundred metres away. Tall and red, it seemingly stood as deserted as the world around it. Vicky pointed at it. "There has to be somewhere we can hide in there. Come on, let's go." She grabbed Flynn's hand and pulled him through the long grass behind her.

The deeper they ran into the field, the longer the grass had grown. Blades whipped against Vicky's face and dragged at her momentum as she tore a path that clearly hadn't been trodden for at least a decade.

Flynn didn't need to be led, so she let go of him and used her hands to push the strong grass aside. The thick stalks left a sting on her palms from where they ripped hundreds of tiny cuts across them.

The screams of the diseased persisted on their heels. Roars and moans followed them, showing the nasty fuckers had clearly picked up their scent.

As they neared the farmhouse, the grass had grown so long Vicky couldn't see their pursuers. She only heard the swish of them drawing closer. By the sound of it, they were gaining on them rapidly.

When Vicky looked up at the farmhouse, the strength drained from her legs. They wouldn't get there before the diseased caught up to them. She looked at Flynn, and her heart ached. The boy trusted her with his life. She'd not steered him wrong yet, but … then she saw it.

Vicky's feet twisted and turned on the uneven ground and the long grass *whooshed* in her ears. A glance at Flynn to make sure he could hear her, and she shouted, "Follow me."

Clearly gassed from the run, Flynn nodded at Vicky but said nothing.

Vicky changed course. Had they not passed so close by then she wouldn't have seen it. A raggedy white shirt on the end of a tall pole, it poked out above the long grass and swayed in the wind. It stood next to the door of what looked like an old storm shelter. A pit in the ground, it had a gate across the front of it. They had no other choice. It had to be the best option. Hopefully, they could get in.

When she caught up to the shelter, Vicky yanked on the black metal gate, and it swung open. The entranceway had been made from concrete, and the gate had a bolt on it. It seemed secure.

As she held the gate open for Flynn, she looked back at the swaying grass. The fuckers wouldn't be able to see them, yet the movement homed in on them anyway. Whatever drove them—scent, sight, or sound—when they focused their attention, it became pretty fucking difficult to lose them.

As Vicky ducked down into the pit after the boy, she pulled

the gate with her. The hinges creaked, and the gate crashed against its concrete frame. The handle of the large bolt hung down, which she slotted home before she backed away just in time for the first of the diseased to reach them. The force with which the lead girl collided with the cage shot her rancid scent into the space and a couple of her teeth flew from her mouth and tinkled on the concrete steps that led down into the hole.

Vicky backed down into the den and watched the girl. The grotesque creature bit at the air between them as she hissed and snarled.

The concrete ended about seven steps down, and it became just a hole in the ground. The reek of damp earth overpowered even the diseased's stench. Just about big enough for her and Flynn, Vicky fought for breath as she looked first at the boy, and then back up at the gathered horde. "At least they can't get to us down here."

"No," Flynn replied, "but they can see us. If they can see us, that means they ain't going anywhere fast."

As Vicky looked up at the gate, she sighed. What little light the small hole let in, got blocked out more and more as the diseased crowded around it. With her world falling into darkness, Vicky sat down, rested her head against one of the muddy walls, and sighed again.

Chapter Forty

It had only been about ten minutes, but it felt like hours had passed. The moisture from the ground had soaked up through Vicky's trousers and knickers, and the pair hadn't spoken since she'd sat down. They stared up the concrete steps at the diseased for the entire time. A jam of faces filled the space, and all of them focused down on her and Flynn.

"What the fuck is this place?" Flynn finally said, his voice deadened by the soft and damp walls.

"I don't know; I really don't." With the time down there, Vicky's eyes had adjusted to the light a little, and she could see better than before. Although crude, she noticed a shelf space had been carved into the wall. It held a book, which she reached out for and grabbed.

A journal of some sort, she couldn't be sure in the poor light, so she shifted around and put her back to the stairs. The gaps in the diseased crush up above let through just enough light for her to read by.

"What is it?" Flynn asked.

"It's a diary." Vicky flicked through the mostly blank book. "Or at least, the start of one."

"What does it say?"

Only a couple of paragraphs long, Vicky read aloud from the book. "*We've been down here for a couple of weeks now. We have nothing to cover the gate with, so the monsters won't leave us alone.*"

"Great," Flynn said.

"*We've been trying to dig our way out, but it's been slow going and we're exhausted.*"

It took for Flynn to point it out before Vicky saw it. "Look, down there."

A tunnel, big enough for an adult to crawl through and no more. Vicky returned to the diary. "*We've left the broken shovel at the end. I hope no one finds themselves down here, but if you do, I pray you manage to dig the rest of the way through. My wife, daughter, and I are all too exhausted to go on. We'll leave now. We plan to open the gate and let the diseased take us. We'll do our best to keep the cage door intact for you. Although I wouldn't wish any time in this dungeon on anyone, I'm afraid to say you're safer here than in the house. We used to live there and there's absolutely nowhere to hide. For that reason, we've made a flag. I'll do my best to stick it in the ground before we're taken down. To anyone who finds this, good luck and God speed.*"

Once she'd finished, Vicky closed the book and looked up at Flynn. The boy watched her with an open mouth and snorted a laugh. "Well, that's cheery."

But Vicky didn't respond. Instead, she dropped down onto her front and crawled into the tunnel.

Although she heard Flynn call to her, "What are you doing?" Vicky ignored him and continued.

The walls seemed to close in around Vicky as she crawled.

Her breaths grew shallow from what felt like a lack of oxygen, but she knew it for the panic it was. Tight spaces did her fucking head in. The damp ground pulled at her clothes and her belt caught some mud and flicked it down the front of her knickers.

Blinded by the darkness, Vicky only knew of the broken spade when she bumped into it. When she gathered it up and stretched it out, it reached the back of the tunnel. One jab of the spade and daylight cut through the gloom. "My God," Vicky whispered. The people had given up just as they would have broken through.

Vicky shifted close to the gap in the wall at the end. She pressed her face into the wet mud and looked out at the diseased beyond. Not many, but because the tunnel came out only about twenty metres away from the entrance to the bunker, there would always be a few stragglers.

***

After she'd crawled backwards down the tunnel, Vicky sat up and drew a deep breath. Once she felt like she'd filled her tight lungs, she turned to the expectant Flynn. "The tunnel's about twenty metres long, and when I jabbed the spade into the wall at the end, I saw daylight.

Flynn gasped. "So we're home free?"

"I saw a few diseased out there, but I reckon I can dig through so the hole's big enough for us to escape, and hopefully we can make it out unseen."

"Let's do it then."

"I need you to stay here."

"*What?*"

"Just for the time being. Let me dig the hole so it's big enough for us to escape from, and you keep the diseased occupied down this end."

"I feel like you're giving me this job to keep me out of the way, Vicky. When will you treat me like an adult? Why don't *you* sit here and do nothing while I go and play the hero down the end of that tunnel."

"I'm not playing the hero, Flynn."

"Whatever. Just do what you need to do down there and you can rely on me to be the good little boy. I'll sit tight and wait it out, yeah?"

"Flynn."

Flynn refused to look at her.

"It's not like that." But it was and they both knew it. Vicky wouldn't trust him to dig them out with the diseased out there. She knew how they reacted so much better than he did. He was just a boy after all. Although she wanted to say something else to him, she knew he'd ignore her. She reached out to pat his shoulder and then stopped. She didn't need to be any more condescending to the poor kid.

Without another word, Vicky shifted off back down the tunnel toward the sliver of daylight at the end.

Chapter Forty-One

Wracked with guilt, but certain in her decision, Vicky reached the end of the tunnel and lifted the broken spade. Flynn would understand when they reached Home. Too heavy-handed with the shovel, and it could fuck everything up. She had to be the one to do it.

Vicky worked the edge of the tool into the gap that let in the light. With the gentlest of movements, she shifted the blade back and forth slowly to increase the size of the hole. Too quick and the diseased may see them.

When she glanced back down the tunnel, she saw Flynn's slumped form at the end. He sat on the bottom stair and looked at the ground while the diseased behind roared and moaned down at him. He'd understand when it all worked out.

As Vicky worked the gap, more daylight spread into her gloomy world. The wet earth, heady in its muddy reek, fell into a small pile. Fuck knows how the family disposed of all the excess mud when they'd dug the hole originally. They must have had to walk up the stairs and throw it out through the gate.

***

After about ten minutes, Vicky had opened up the hole big enough that the smell of the diseased overpowered the reek of wet earth. A good sign because it meant they could run now. When she peered out of her foxhole, she looked at the diseased as they milled about. With about twenty of the fuckers in her line of sight, who knew how many more hid beyond her vision.

A barn stood about fifty metres away. Old, wooden, and black, if they could use that for shelter, it would take them one step farther away from the horrible fuckers.

When Vicky looked back down the tunnel, she made eye contact with Flynn. She raised her thumb at him, and the boy smiled at her. They were home free. They'd make it.

As quietly as she could, Vicky whispered to Flynn, "Make some noise so you pull the diseased around to your side. Maybe take the spear up there and attack some of them."

The boy nodded and walked up the concrete steps. As he moved closer, it whipped the diseased into a frenzy. Not that Vicky could see them, but she heard the sounds of agitation, and she listened to the gate rattle in its concrete frame.

A glance outside and she watched the head of every diseased within her line of sight prick up. Within no time, they'd all moved away from her side of the hole. They would have to be quick when Flynn reached her. Hopefully, the diseased would watch Flynn disappear, and it would make them more interested in staring down into the den.

It seemed clear outside of the hole, so Vicky poked her head up and looked around. She withdrew almost instantly. Although she saw some diseased, they all had their attention focused on the gate at the front. So many of them gathered around the hole that Vicky and Flynn wouldn't be able to fight them; spear or not.

When she ducked back down, she found Flynn staring at her. He held onto his spear with both hands and looked out of breath. "Good work, Flynn. Well done. I think we've got this." With a beckoning hand, she called him toward her. "Let's get the fuck out of here."

As Flynn moved up the tunnel, the sound of the diseased chased down it after him. With concentration locking his face tight, he made it about halfway down before it happened.

At first, just a scattering of mud fell to the ground. Nothing much, and bound to happen in a tunnel like that, right? But even that caught Vicky's attention, and her heart leaped in her chest.

Another metre farther down and more dirt fell from the ceiling. Still only a handful, but enough. Flynn had seen it too this time, and he looked straight at Vicky.

"Come on," she whispered as she beckoned him toward her again. "You can do it."

Flynn picked his pace up and moved up the tunnel with more urgency. When a lump of dirt fell on his head and broke over his crown, Vicky's chest tightened, and her pulse ran away with her. Before she could say anything else, everything slipped into what felt like slow motion.

First, the mud behind the boy rained down as the tunnel collapsed. Not only did it block his retreat, but it rushed up and over the back of his legs. Such a large amount of earth, Flynn looked up at Vicky. "I'm trapped. Help!"

Before Vicky could react, the earth above the boy fell onto his back and surrounded him.

"Vicky," Flynn called out and reached for her. A second later, the dirt covered him.

As much as Vicky wanted to cry out to the boy, she held it in her throat and watched on, her jaw slack, her stomach turning backflips. His outstretched hand remained the only visible part of him, but even that vanished a few seconds later as the earth smothered it.

Vicky scrambled away from the rush of mud and dirt so it didn't trap her too. She jumped out of the hole to see the diseased remained focused on the gate. In one final futile attempt, she reached into the hole. The earth had fallen in such a quantity, she'd have to dig to get him out. With the broken spade buried with the boy, she'd have no fucking hope with just her hands. Another glance at the pack of diseased and she backed away.

The long grass pulled on Vicky's forward momentum, but she gritted her teeth and pushed on. She didn't look back. Not yet. Until she got to the barn, she couldn't do anything else.

***

Once she'd gotten to the barn and ducked around the side of it, Vicky stood with her back pressed into the wood, breathless and with her pulse running away with her. The place seemed free of diseased.

The tunnel had closed in from both ends and trapped Flynn. No way would he make it out alive. When Vicky glanced back around the barn, she saw more diseased head over to the gate, although they already seemed less agitated. Whatever they had been able to see had clearly gone.

With a lump like broken glass in her throat, Vicky watched the diseased and the filled-in hole she'd escaped from. No way would Flynn have survived that. No fucking way. Vicky's world blurred with her tears. If only she'd let him lead the way from the tunnel. He'd now be the one outside by the barn.

The hot rush of grief turned Vicky's cheeks damp as she looked up at the sky. Would Rhys and Larissa be looking down at that moment? After all the time she'd spent convincing Rhys to treat his son like a young man, she'd treated him like a child at the very end. Because she didn't take her own fucking advice, she'd sentenced the boy to death.

Vicky watched the filled-in hole for a little longer. Maybe a hand would appear through it. Although, if she couldn't dig into the wet mud, there's no way Flynn would be able to dig his way out. He was lost, and the sooner she accepted it, the better. She couldn't fight the diseased to dig his body out. She had to go to Home and come back when the monsters had moved on. She'd find his corpse then and give him the burial he deserved.

Weighted with depression, Vicky turned her back on the shelter and trudged across the field in the direction of Home, her face sodden with tears, her vision blurred to the point where she could barely see a metre in front of her.

Chapter Forty-Two

Vicky gripped her telescopic baton so tightly, her knuckles hurt. Exhausted, hungry, thirsty, and broken, she pushed on as she ran down the cracked road. Maybe she could go back to Flynn at some point. She could get safely away and then find some way to return and take his body. His parents would want him to be buried properly. She owed them that at least.

Like most of the roads she'd travelled—certainly the ones outside of the city—the road she currently ran down looked like it would be claimed by nature soon enough. Before long, the entire area would be nothing but fields of long grass. Although, not the patchwork ridiculousness that used to pass as nature; these would be proper fields, without boundaries and human management. But for now, it still provided something to run on.

As Vicky jogged—clumsy with every step she took—she scanned the space in front of her. The last sign about five hundred metres back had explained Home was just over the river. Except, she hadn't seen the river yet.

When Vicky heard the familiar beat of clumsy footsteps, she

spun around. One diseased man, he fixed her with their signature stare—bloody and full of rage—as he bore down on her.

"Fuck this." Vicky stopped and turned to face the creature.

With her baton pulled back, she clenched her jaw and screamed as she swung for the fucker. The balled end of the baton caught it on the top of its head with a *crack*. A vibration ran down the handle and drove a deep dent into the diseased's skull.

Vicky jumped aside to stop the horrible fucker grabbing her as it passed. Before it could turn around, she ran after it and cracked it over the back of the head this time. The blow turned the creature's legs bandy, and it folded to the floor in a heap.

When Vicky raised her baton to finish the creature off, she heard it; the call of the diseased. Maybe ten, maybe one hundred. However many had picked up her tail, from the sound of them, Vicky wouldn't be able to fight them off. She spat at the downed diseased at her feet and took off down the road.

As always, the diseased had the beating of her, but Vicky pushed on. The sign had mentioned a river …

Panting from the run, Vicky reached the river as the diseased came into view. The large flowing body of water sat at least ten metres wide, and it had no bridge. Or, at least, no bridge that Vicky could see. Thank God!

Without a break in stride, Vicky headed straight for the rushing water and leaped into it. She kept a hold of her baton as she swam across the gap.

So deep her feet didn't touch the ground, Vicky pushed on across the rushing water, the tide strong enough to carry her with it as she made her way across.

When she climbed out on the other side, Vicky turned to look at the crowd she'd left behind. They'd gathered at the river's edge, and all stared across at her. A strange calm occupied their twisted faces; an acceptance that they'd lost this one, despite their desire to get at her.

As the riverbank on the opposite side filled up, Vicky shook her head and a deep depression tugged on her frame along with her damp clothes. She couldn't go back for Flynn's body; it would be suicide.

Chapter Forty-Three

Soaked from the river, Vicky's shoes squelched as she walked through the field on the other side. Downwind from the diseased she'd left behind, she may not have been able to see them anymore, but she remained aware of their presence through the soured air that surrounded her. As she walked away, their distant groans and moans accompanied her.

The fight had damn near left Vicky as she trudged through the long grass. Each step drained her already exhausted frame, and she lost focus several times.

When she'd climbed out of the river, she'd been in a field, but it didn't take long for her to find the road again—or what remained of it anyway. The river must have had a bridge across it at some point. The people from Home probably destroyed it on purpose. God knows Vicky would have done the same in their situation; anything to gain an advantage over the diseased.

A large sign protruded from the ground. At first, Vicky couldn't read the words. She was so exhausted, the text sat as a blurred mess for her. After repeated blinks, Vicky rubbed her eyes and read it. WELCOME TO HOME. Unlike the other sign she'd seen with Flynn, this one had been kept in better condition.

Vicky stared at the sign and swayed with exhaustion. The cold water that soaked her clothes seemed to treble her weight, although the dampness inside of her heart overpowered any physical effects from the river. Now she'd gotten to Home, she didn't give a fuck. After losing Flynn, nothing mattered anymore.

The large red arrow on the sign pointed down the road, so Vicky followed it, her heavy footsteps scraping over the rough ground. What would Flynn's final moments have been like? Hopefully it ended quickly for him. He may have gotten out to be attacked by the diseased, although more than likely, he suffocated beneath the heavy weight of damp earth. Vicky shook her head. It served no purpose to think about it. Flynn had died, and Vicky could have been there instead of him had she trusted his ability. Instead, she sentenced him to death.

As Vicky rounded the next corner, she saw it. Nothing more than one storey high and about the width of an average house, a box of a building sat in the middle of a field. It had a steel door at the front with a window on either side of it, and grass grew over the entire thing. Were it not for the door and windows, it would have looked like a mound of earth.

Vicky froze and she stared at the building in front of her. The broadcasts had made it sound like something far grander. A couple of days' walk and the loss of three people she loved, for this?

When the sound of two huge steel bolts snapped through the relative silence, Vicky raised both hands in the air and waited.

Whatever this place was, she'd arrived, so she needed to see it through.

Two men stepped out through the door. Dressed from head to toe in army gear, they both wore masks, and they each carried a shotgun. With their weapons raised, they stepped toward Vicky.

Vicky's pulse raced as she stared at the men. Although imposing, she turned away from them to watch her surroundings in case of diseased.

As the men drew closer, Vicky saw that they too had their attention on their surroundings rather than her. The pair walked past her and continued to look around. One of the men, his voice muffled by his mask, said to Vicky, "Follow us back in. We've got your back."

The two men walked backwards toward Home, their guns raised the entire time. When they drew closer to the door, Vicky saw it had been locked again. The same two snaps cut through the relative silence and the hinges on the door creaked as someone pulled it open.

"You go first, love," one of the men said to Vicky.

Once inside, a third man slammed the large steel door with a *crash* that damn near lifted Vicky's feet from the ground as it startled her. Vicky looked around. A foyer, it had a flight of stairs at each end that led down into what seemed to be a complex far grander than its external appearance suggested.

With everyone inside, the third man dragged the large bolts back across to secure the door.

The two armed men both put their guns down and pulled off their masks. One of the men, a dark-haired fellow in what seemed to be his early forties, held his hand out to Vicky. With a bright smile and a glint in his eyes, he said, "Hi, I'm Hugh. Welcome to Home."

The ball of grief inside of Vicky popped, and her sadness rushed out of her in a hot mess of tears, sobs, and wails. A second later, her legs gave way beneath her, and she hit the ground hard.

Chapter Forty-Four

A headache sat as a sharp pain behind Vicky's eyeballs, and her temples throbbed. The bed may have been soft beneath her, but her body ached like she had blood poisoning.

It took several groans before Vicky could even think about moving. She finally sat upright in bed. The mattress may have been cleaner and softer than anything she'd slept on in a long time, but as Vicky looked around the room, she couldn't ignore the fact that she currently sat in what appeared to be a locked cell. "What the fuck," she muttered as she scratched her head.

The small space—a windowless box a couple of metres square—had a strip light that ran across the ceiling. A bed and nothing else in the room, it had stark white walls. Aesthetically cold if nothing else, a chill snapped through Vicky as she took the place in.

The door to the cell looked like something from medieval times. Made from thick wood, it had a small hole as a window no more than the size of a shoebox. Black bars ran vertically across it. Before she could get to her feet, Vicky saw the plate on the floor. It had a sandwich on it. Vicky picked it up and inhaled the smell of fresh bread and cheese. Her hunger damn near beat its way from her body to get to the snack. First, Vicky picked the bottle of water up and took a sip. Cool and refreshing, she let the liquid rehydrate her parched throat.

Vicky salivated as she bit into the sandwich and smelled the mix of bread, butter, and cheese. The salty taste of the cheese stretched through her mouth and she groaned. Fuck knows why she found herself in a cell at that moment, but if they gave her food like this, they could keep her in here forever.

After she'd washed down her first mouthful with a gulp of water, a lock snapped free on the other side of her cell door and Vicky looked up to watch it open.

Despite the uncertainty of what could come through, Vicky took another bite of the sandwich. Whatever happened to her, it would happen with food in her stomach.

Hugh, the man who'd let her into Home, walked in with a woman. The guy seemed friendly, but Vicky said nothing to him. Dressed in grey tracksuit bottoms and a loose t-shirt, Hugh smiled at her. Thick biceps poked out of the bottom of his sleeves, and his pecs lifted the rest of the t-shirt away from his stomach.

"How are you doing?" Hugh asked. "I'm—"

"Hugh, I know. You said that the first time we met."

"I didn't know if you'd have remembered."

Vicky stared at him.

"You're probably wondering why we have you locked up?"

Vicky continued to stare.

"Wow, tough crowd."

"Your prisoners are normally a laugh a minute then?"

After a slight pause, Hugh laughed. "Fair point. Look …"

"Vicky."

"Vicky. Look, Vicky, let me cut to the chase. Home is a friendly place and we welcome anyone who shares our vision. We're surviving, and we're doing it well, but we want to take this world back. We don't have enough people yet, but more are coming all the time. We hope to form an army formidable enough to go to war against the diseased."

Vicky scoffed. "You realise that most of the country have turned into those things, right?"

"You've been around the entire country?"

With her jaw clenched, Vicky watched the man in front of her. "All right, smart arse, but you shouldn't underestimate the task you have ahead of you."

"I don't. But every diseased we kill is one less in the country, right?"

The woman who'd entered with Hugh hadn't spoken. Vicky looked at her, and the woman looked back. Arched eyebrows and a severe ponytail, the woman had a face that pulled back with her tight hair. She shrugged and looked back at Hugh.

When Hugh sat down next to Vicky on the bed, she caught a whiff of the guy for the first time. A clean mix of soap and flowers, Vicky shifted away from him. She probably stank in comparison. "We quarantine everyone that comes into Home for the first two days. If you haven't turned by then, you're given a bed to stay in and welcomed into the community with open arms. We normally explain that to someone when they arrive, but with you collapsing, we had to assume your consent."

"And if I reject your terms now?"

"Then you can leave. No harm, no foul."

Vicky didn't respond.

"We have about one hundred people here already, Vicky. We'd love for you to join our ever-expanding community."

The way Hugh looked at Vicky—his dark eyes staring directly into hers—spread heat through her cheeks, and although she wanted to reply this time, she couldn't find the words. Instead, she simply stared back and her throat dried. She hadn't been looked at in that way for a long time.

Although she gulped, it had little effect, and before she could say anything, Hugh picked up the water bottle from the floor and handed it to her. "Here." He smiled again.

A shake ran through Vicky's hands as she fumbled with the bottle cap. After she'd finally managed to remove it, she took a sip and drew several deep breaths.

Before she could speak, Hugh got to his feet. "We'll bring you regular food and water, but please shout if you need *anything*. Someone will hear you and bring you what you need; if we can provide it, that is. Now, I hope you don't mind, but Jessica here will need to inspect you for bites and cuts. I'm sure you're fine; it's just a formality, you know?"

Because he hadn't asked for her permission, Vicky didn't give it. They would do what they wanted to, and what Hugh said made sense. They'd survived this long for a reason.

For the first time since she'd entered the room, Jessica smiled at Vicky. As Hugh walked out, she said, "Now, if you'd please stand up and remove your clothes."

Vicky did as the woman asked her. As she unzipped her coat,

she watched Hugh leave the cell. The guy didn't look back once. The perfect gentleman. Were the roles reversed, Vicky would have found it damn hard not to get an eyeful of his naked form.

Chapter Forty-Five

Although Hugh opened the door and walked into her cell with a broad smile on his face, Vicky remained on the mattress and stared at the man. Neither hungry nor thirsty anymore, she had little motivation to move and her body had turned to lead.

"Come on then," Hugh said, "you've done your time. Let's get you out of here."

"Do I have to?"

"Huh?"

Vicky sighed and dropped her head back against the pillow. "I've had a decade of looking after people; of sleeping on a cold and hard floor; of existing day to day. I could get used to sleeping all day and having someone wait on me hand and foot."

Hugh laughed. "You and I both know you'd get bored."

After she'd shrugged, Vicky sat up. "Yeah, you're right." When she dropped her feet down onto the hard floor, the coldness of it stretched up through her exposed soles and banished her lethargy. During her stay, she'd been given fresh clothes and clean water to bathe in. Other than a dip in the river near to the airport, or a rainwater shower in the bathroom container, she'd not had a decent wash for the longest time. Despite the bitterness attached to her memories of her journey, coming to Home looked like it had been one of her better decisions in the past decade.

***

Because she'd been unconscious when they took her to her cell, Vicky hadn't seen much of Home. The holding cell existed on a long corridor full of identically sized rooms. Some had doors like the room she'd stayed in, while others had none at all and looked like they were used for storage. Strip lighting ran along the ceiling in the hallway, providing the same unnatural glare that she'd experienced in her cell. They'd asked her if she wanted the light on at night. No thank you! She may have had nightmares in the darkness, but at least she slept.

At the end of the corridor, they came to a huge open space. Easily big enough for three football fields, maybe four, a large part of it had been sectioned off and contained an industrial kitchen. In another corner stood a medical bay, not that it looked terribly well equipped. No doubt countless people had died in those beds as the community tried to save them. She didn't need to ask for Hugh's confirmation on that.

The crash of pots and crockery filled the air, and Vicky flinched several times as the bangs rang hard enough to drive needles into her eardrums.

After two days of solitary incarceration, the activity in the place sent Vicky's head into a spin. She shut down to her environment as much as she could and focused on Hugh's broad back as he led them from the huge area.

As if stuck on a loop, the next corridor they entered looked exactly the same as the one with the holding cells, except every room had a door on it. Each room looked the same—or at least the ones Vicky could see into did.

Small like the holding cell, each room had a bed in the middle. Instead of the hard industrial floor, these rooms had rugs and carpets. "This is where you'll sleep," Hugh said when he stopped outside one of the rooms.

After she'd dropped a sharp nod to the man, Vicky walked past him and entered the room.

Before she could sit on the bed, Hugh said, "It's morning. Will you come to the canteen with me for breakfast?"

The sound of the kitchen had been bad enough. The chaos of a canteen could drive her over the edge. But Vicky didn't voice her feelings. Instead, she nodded at Hugh and followed him along the corridor.

The room at the end bore a striking resemblance to the kitchen and medical area. Similar in dimensions, this space had rows and rows of tables. People sat at the tables. More people than Vicky had seen in the past ten years.

They had kids there too. The little scamps tore around, food in their mouths and their parents' voices chasing behind them. How lovely to see such abandon in the children. Flynn lost that years ago. To even think about the boy ran a shredding pain through Vicky's throat.

When Vicky sat down, Hugh plonked himself on the bench opposite her. "So," he said, "breakfast?"

Vicky nodded.

Hugh smiled at her. "I'll go and get you some."

***

It may have been powdered milk, but Vicky hadn't tasted cereal in a long time. Fuck knows what they called the small wheat-based biscuits, but they had clearly been grown and processed by the community. Not that delicious needed a name. Vicky lifted another spoon to her mouth and crunched down on the sweet cereal.

With Hugh opposite her, Vicky did her best to ignore him. So when he spoke to her, her heart sank. She needed time to acclimatise to the place. Didn't he get that?

"So how did you end up at Home?"

The roof caved in again in Vicky's mind and she watched the boy she loved like a son die all over again. A thick frown darkened her view of the world in front of her, and Vicky directed it at Hugh.

"Whoa," Hugh said, "I'm only asking the single most popular question you'll get while you're here.

Well, maybe she didn't want to answer it, and maybe Hugh should respect that.

Each wall in the canteen had a huge monitor on it. Each screen showed the same footage. It cycled through what must have been external cameras, one after the other. When she looked back at Hugh, she found him staring at her.

"We have those monitors up," Hugh said, "to remind us what's outside of our safe walls."

At that moment, a group of four diseased people appeared on one of the cameras. Everyone stopped to watch them. The children booed and hissed.

"Yet, you've probably desensitised the people to the horrors by turning it into a movie," Vicky said. "Show them a shocking image enough times, especially when it's diluted by being on a screen, and it won't be shocking anymore. You're not toughening these kids up; you're turning them into weaklings that won't fear what is the most credible threat to their existence."

Although Hugh opened his mouth to reply, Vicky turned away from him and focused on her breakfast. The burn of his attention itched into the side of her face until, eventually, he focused on his breakfast too.

Chapter Forty-Six

The dark meat had a rich taste that seeped into the gravy and through the veg. Vicky didn't want to seem ungrateful, and she wouldn't have called the flavour unpleasant, but had they given her a menu, she certainly wouldn't have ordered it.

As she chewed on the meat, Vicky looked up at Hugh again. "What is this?"

"Stew."

After Vicky had looked down at it for a second, she looked back at him. "I can see that, but what *kind* of stew?"

"Oh, I'd say probably squirrel. I'm not sure. I'm not a member of the hunting party, so half the time I don't know." He smiled. "As long as it ain't human, eh?"

The smell of the burned man returned to Vicky's nostrils and she looked away from Hugh. He had no way of knowing what she'd been through. How could he?

Another mouthful of squirrel and Vicky looked around the canteen again. Flynn would have loved the stew. The boy ate anything, and to be fair to him, he probably could have made it taste better than those in Home's kitchen had. They'd gotten so close to freedom to fuck it up at the last minute. Poor kid. Vicky drew a heavy sigh. It did nothing to relieve the weight on her sore heart.

As she chewed on her food, Vicky watched the monitors in the canteen. The grass swayed as if of its own accord, the huge blades dancing as one. Like the children who had turned the diseased into pantomime villains, Vicky watched the outside world as if it didn't exist as a reality beyond their walls.

When the grass on one of the cameras moved slightly differently to all of the others, Vicky got to her feet.

With her eyes fixed on the monitor, she felt Hugh look up at her. "Are you okay?"

Vicky squinted as she watched the screen and said nothing to the man next to her. Then she caught a glimpse of it and her heart lifted. A dirty form, covered in mud, it walked like a human, not a diseased.

Vicky kicked her seat back and it crashed to the floor. A busy canteen, Vicky could feel all the sets of eyes on her as she rushed over to the screen and stared up at it. Maybe they thought the new girl had gone feral. They were bound to have seen the newest arrivals pop when the pressure of the outside world had been taken off them.

Just a metre from one of the monitors, Vicky stared at it. A sharp sting itched her eyes as she watched on without blinking. From years of existing out in the open, she knew how to spot signs of movement in the grass. Hell, she even knew how it looked when the movement had been caused by a diseased.

Another glance at the form in the grass and her heart jumped. As Hugh joined her by her side, she spoke frantic words, her lungs tight from the excitement. "It's him, Hugh."

"Who?"

"Flynn."

"Who the fuck's Flynn?"

"My so—" But he wasn't her son. "My ... um, my travelling partner. I thought I'd lost him."

Without another word, Vicky sprinted off through the canteen. She swerved through the tables and chairs and ignored the people that stared at her. Of course they would stare at her. But fuck them. Somehow, against all the odds, Flynn had survived.

Chapter Forty-Seven

Once Vicky had exited the canteen, she sprinted down a corridor that looked exactly like the others that had her holding cell and new room on.

She didn't look back, but she heard Hugh's footsteps as he chased after her. "Vicky," he called. "Wait up, don't do anything stupid."

Stupid? She'd written Flynn off before he'd been killed. She'd already done something stupid; now she needed to make amends.

After a couple of days' rest and some food, she moved more easily than she had in years. The aches and pains that characterised every movement had gone. She could run forever if she needed to. Strong again, she pushed on as she passed people's private living quarters on either side of the long hall.

The stairs at the end looked familiar. When Vicky reached them, she bounded to the top in three long strides and came out in the first room she'd come to when they let her into Home. A large steel door with a window on either side, Vicky pressed her face against the cold glass and stared out.

Although her quick breaths steamed up her view of the outside world, she saw the boy approach. He'd gotten to within twenty metres of the complex. Vicky reached up and grabbed the large bolt at the top of the door. She slid it across with a loud *crack* and did the same for the bottom one.

Hugh had shouted something, but she hadn't heard it. By the time he'd reached the door, she'd already burst free of the complex and sprinted out across the long grass.

Vicky waved her hands above her head as she ran. "Flynn! Flynn!"

The bedraggled boy looked at her; his shoulders slumped, his clothes filthy, a broken spear in his hand. The slightest twitch of a smile lifted on his face as Vicky continued to sprint toward him.

When she reached him, she fought for breath and pulled on his arm. Mud clung to the boy from head to toe, clearly from where he'd been buried. Tears burned Vicky's eyes as she stared at him. "I'm so sorry. I'm so sorry I left you. I thought you'd died." When she hugged him, it filled her senses with the reek of damp earth. "I'm so sorry."

The scream of the diseased cut through their reunion, and when Vicky looked up, she saw several of the horrible fuckers come around the bend and head toward them. A tug on Flynn's arm and she led him back toward Home.

Hugh stopped in his tracks when he saw them run back, turned around, and led the retreat to the complex.

A few seconds after Hugh ran through the door, Vicky dragged Flynn in with her.

Hugh locked them in, the diseased getting closer with every second.

After he'd secured the first bolt, a loud *bang* exploded through the small foyer and the bottom half of the door came away from its frame for a second. With his weight against the steel barrier, Hugh slid the other bolt home. The next *bang* had little impact on the secured door.

Vicky breathed a relieved sigh and looked at Flynn again. Tears turned her world blurry, but she tried to look at the boy anyway. Her words croaked when she said, "You're okay! You're okay!"

Despite her poor vision, she saw the smile on Flynn's face. "Of course I'm okay. I'm not the kid you think I am."

Vicky smiled through her tears and hugged Flynn again. Now she'd gotten herself clean, she suddenly realised just how bad Flynn smelled. A mixture of mud and ground-in dirt, he stank like an old bog. Vicky pulled away and laughed. "You need a bath."

When he laughed too, Vicky balked at the alien sound. It had been a long time since she'd heard him happy like that. She cried harder than before and then took the boy's hands in hers. As she drank in the sight she thought she'd lost forever, she said, "We made it, mate."

When they pressed their foreheads against one another's, Vicky watched Flynn's tears fall to the ground. He drew a deep and stuttered breath and said, "We made it."

Ends.

Thank you for reading The Alpha Plague 4

The Alpha Plague 5 is avaialble now at
www.michaelrobertson.co.uk

If you would like to receive special offers and news on all of my new releases, join my spam-free mailing list here:-
www.michaelrobertson.co.uk

Support the Author

Dear reader, as an independent author I don't have the resources of a huge publisher. If you like my work and would like to see more from me in the future, there are two things you can do to help: leaving a review, and a word-of-mouth referral.

Releasing a book takes many hours and hundreds of dollars. I love to write, and would love to continue to do so. All I ask is that you leave an Amazon review. It shows other readers that you've enjoyed the book and will encourage them to give it a try too. The review can be just one sentence, or as long as you like.

Other Works Available by Michael Robertson

The Shadow Order - Available Now:

New Reality: Truth - Available now for FREE:

Crash - Available now for FREE:

Rat Run - Available Now:

For a list and links of all of my titles - go to
www.michaelrobertson.co.uk

About The Author

Michael Robertson has been a writer for many years and has had poetry and short stories published, most notably with HarperCollins. He first discovered his desire to write as a skinny weed-smoking seventeen-year-old badman who thought he could spit bars over drum and bass. Fortunately, that venture never left his best mate's bedroom and only a few people had to endure his musical embarrassment. He hasn't so much as looked at a microphone since. What the experience taught him was that he liked to write. So that's what he did.

After sending poetry to countless publications and receiving MANY rejection letters, he uttered the words, "That's it, I give up." The very next day, his first acceptance letter arrived in the post. He saw it as a sign that he would find his way in the world as a writer.

Over a decade and a half later, he now has a young family to inspire him and has decided to follow his joy with every ounce of his being. With the support of his amazing partner, Amy, he's managed to find the time to take the first step of what promises to be an incredible journey. Love, hope, and the need to eat get him out of bed every morning to spend a precious few hours pursuing his purpose.

If you want to connect with Michael:

Subscribe to my newsletter at –
www.michaelrobertson.co.uk

Email me at –
subscribers@michaelrobertson.co.uk

Follow me on Facebook at –
www.facebook.com/MichaelRobertsonAuthor

Twitter at –
@MicRobertson

Google Plus at –
plus.google.com/u/0/113009673177382863155/posts

OTHER AUTHORS UNDER THE SHIELD OF

SIXTH CYCLE

Nuclear war has destroyed human civilization.
Captain Jake Phillips wakes into a dangerous new world, where he finds the remaining fragments of the population living in a series of strongholds, connected across the country. Uneasy alliances have maintained their safety, but things are about to change. — Discovery **leads to danger.** — Skye Reed, a tracker from the Omega stronghold, uncovers a threat that could spell the end for their fragile society. With friends and enemies revealing truths about the past, she will need to decide who to trust. — **Sixth Cycle** is a gritty post-apocalyptic story of survival and adventure.

Darren Wearmouth ~ Carl Sinclair

DEAD ISLAND: Operation Zulu

Ten years after the world was nearly brought to its knees by a zombie Armageddon, there is a race for the antidote! On a remote Caribbean island, surrounded by a horde of hungry living dead, a team of American and Australian commandos must rescue the Antidotes' scientist. Filled with zombies, guns, Russian bad guys, shady government types, serial killers and elevator muzak. Dead Island is an action packed blood soaked horror adventure.

Allen Gamboa

INVASION OF THE DEAD SERIES

This is the first book in a series of nine, about an ordinary bunch of friends, and their plight to survive an apocalypse in Australia. — Deep beneath defense headquarters in the Australian Capital Territory, the last ranking Army chief and a brilliant scientist struggle with answers to the collapse of the world, and the aftermath of an unprecedented virus. Is it a natural mutation, or does the infection contain — more sinister roots? — One hundred and fifty miles away, five friends returning from a month-long camping trip slowly discover that death has swept through the country. What greets them in a gradual revelation is an enemy beyond compare. — Armed with dwindling ammunition, the friends must overcome their disagreements, utilize their individual skills, and face unimaginable horrors as they battle to reach their hometown…

Owen Baillie

WHISKEY TANGO FOXTROT

Alone in a foreign land. The radio goes quiet while on convoy in Afghanistan, a lost patrol alone in the desert. With his unit and his home base destroyed, Staff Sergeant Brad Thompson suddenly finds himself isolated and in command of a small group of men trying to survive in the Afghan wasteland. **Every turn leads to danger**

The local population has been afflicted with an illness that turns them into rabid animals. They pursue him and his men at every corner and stop. Struggling to hold his team together and unite survivors, he must fight and evade his way to safety.

A fast paced zombie war story like no other.

W.J. Lundy

ZOMBIE RUSH

New to the Hot Springs PD Lisa Reynolds was not all that welcomed by her coworkers especially those who were passed over for the position. It didn't matter, her thirty days probation ended on the same day of the Z-poc's arrival. Overnight the world goes from bad to worse as thousands die in the initial onslaught. National Guard and regular military unit deployed the day before to the north leaves the city in mayhem. All directions lead to death until one unlikely candidate steps forward with a plan. A plan that became an avalanche raging down the mountain culminating in the salvation or destruction of them all.

Joseph Hansen

THE GATHERING HORDE

The most ambitious terrorist plot ever undertaken is about to be put into motion, releasing an unstoppable force against humanity. Ordinary people – A group of students celebrating the end of the semester, suburban and rural families – are about to themselves in the center of something that threatens the survival of the human species. As they battle the dead – and the living – it's going to take every bit of skill, knowledge and luck for them to survive in Zed's World.

Rich Baker

THE FORGOTTEN LAND

Sergeant Steve Golburn, an Australian Special Air Service veteran, is tasked with a dangerous mission in Iraq, deep behind enemy lines. When Steve's five man SAS patrol inadvertently spark a time portal, they find themselves in 10th century Viking Denmark. A place far more dangerous and lawless than modern Iraq. Join the SAS patrol on this action adventure into the depths of not only a hostile land, far away from the support of the Allied front line, but into another world…another time.

Keith McArdle

<<<<>>>>

Printed in Great Britain
by Amazon